Gentlemen and Fortune

Edited by Jeff Byrne

To the
Pirate Wulff

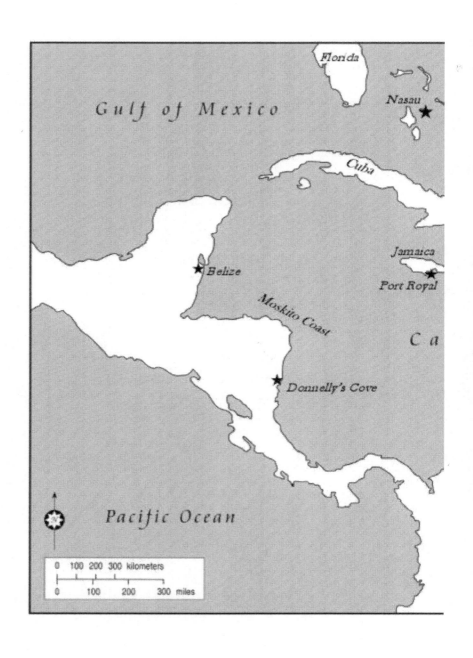

Atlantic Ocean
Bahama Islands
Greater Antilles
Hispaniola
Puerto Rico
Lesser Antilles
Montserrat
ribbean Sea
Martinique
Barbados
Maracaibo
Spanish Main

Scarlet Sails

"Where's the bloody payroll?"

Scarlet MacGrath strode from the ruin of the captain's cabin, grabbed the schooner's captain by the front of his shirt and dug the muzzle of her flintlock pistol into the flesh of the man's face, up under the cheekbone. The white of his eye rolled upward. They stood against each other for a long moment, and finally he said, steady enough, "There ain't no payroll, the men are in on shares."

She backed off then, half a thoughtful step, leaving the print of her pistol barrel on his cheek, and asked a little more politely, "What are you meanin' by that?"

"I own the boat. I suspected the merchant houses of cheating us, so it bein' the off season, I told the boys that any man who came south with me would have a percentage. I was aimin' to sell in Jamaica."

She lowered the pistol and gave him a little more space. "Well, I have a great respect for a man what treats his crew fair. We'll still rob you, mind, but I will apologize about your cabin." Litter from her search was visible through the open door, clothing and books scattered, the desk overturned, the sea chest rifled, the bunk torn apart.

1

Scarlet put the pistol away in her coat pocket and turned to her quartermaster. Burgess had just come up from below decks, and stood polishing his steel-rimmed glasses. "Captain MacGrath. I've seen the cargo. It's just as the men say, forty tons of salt cod, no more no less, and not a penny's worth of other cargo aboard her."

"You see, we're no treasure ship. Will you let us go now?" the schooner's captain asked, rubbing the mark on his cheek.

Scarlet ran a hand through her long red hair and laughed. "Do you think we only look for Spanish gold? If we held out for that we'd starve, sure as sure as sunrise. No, cod's good enough for us. Mister Burgess, how much can we take on?"

Burgess took the big brown ledger from under his arm and consulted it. "Three tons I should say, Captain."

"Three tons it is. Kindly ask Mister Flynn if he will rig the cargo crane, and we'll bring it over easy." She spared an affectionate glance to her own *Donnybrook,* bobbing alongside the schooner; sixty five feet of deck, ten guns, and Mister Bracegirdle hanging about them, still hoping for an excuse to fire.

Scarlet turned back to the schooner captain. "I've just one more thing to ask, but if you answer true, I'll make it worth your while."

The man still rubbed thoughtfully at his cheek, but his eyes traveled up and down Scarlet's body. She did not make a display of bosom, but her shirt fit her close and she had, as usual, pinned her skirts up nearly to the knee, showing her sea-boots. She let him look for a moment, laughed again and said, "Not that. I mean to offer you information. That is free and won't delay our parting."

"Well then, ask."

"How much liquor on board?"

"We've two barrels of cider left."

"Well, I will take one of them. And here's your gift. Don't sell in Jamaica. That's a colony of England, and England claims all them northern fishing banks. Your cod merchants may have purchased some sort of monopoly from the Crown. If they have, and they notice you selling, they'll seize your cargo and fine you or jail you or both."

"Damn. You may be right. This long old trip for nothing."

"That ain't what I said. Where you should sell is the island north, Cuba. The Spanish love cod, and they'll pay dear, for they don't own any cod banks."

A slow, sly smile came into the sloop captain's eyes. Then he looked sharp at Scarlet. "And will you be selling my fish there, too?"

She looked out at the horizon. "Cuba's a little... warm for us right now. We'll find a buyer. Everyone wants the stuff, and I don't need to bother about the price. If we can't sell we won't go hungry. My navigator will tell you what you need to know." She called out to the *Donny's* quarterdeck. "Pryce!"

The man beside her stared for a moment, his expression half annoyance, half curiosity. "I never thought I'd take advice from someone robbing me. What's in it for you?"

Scarlet grinned. "I enjoy fekkin' with rich merchant houses. You may not know, but there's three rules to pirating in these waters. Take what you want. Get away with it. Have a good time." She headed toward the rail, then paused and looked back. "Welcome to the Caribbean."

⌘

Three hours later, with the cod safely stowed and the schooner falling away behind them, Scarlet stood out on the *Donnybrook's* quarterdeck and called "Ship's meeting! Gather up!"

In only a few moments the sixty-odd members of the crew had assembled, a motley mix of men and women, young and old. Most were dressed in stolen finery, all carried scars of one sort or another. No one became a pirate because they were doing too well at life.

When she had everyone's attention Scarlet cleared her throat. "Listen up. You likely know already, but we ain't been finding much liquor on our prizes. We've food enough, water enough, but the grog just ain't been coming in, and them barrels of wine we took last week had turned to vinegar in the casks."

A low murmur. Sunny Jim raised his voice in alarm. "We're out of grog!"

Burgess stepped forward, neat and tidy in his olive green suit, glasses polished and book clutched in his arms, looking more like a shopkeeper than a pirate. Scarlet shouted down the unhappy mutters and motioned for him to speak. "We are not out of anything. If we went on rations like sensible folk we should last a week. But guzzle it down, and it won't last three days."

Before true alarm could spread Scarlet raised her voice again. "We just took on three tons of salt cod. Someone will be willing to make a trade. What we need to do is choose a port, go in and barter. We should have no trouble."

"Providence!" called Dark Maire, her scarred face brightening into a smile.

"Jamaica!" shouted Flynn.

"Aye! Port Royal!"

"Port Royal?" Scarlet asked, scorn in her voice. "And them with a fine new governor, all fresh from England with a license to hunt pirates? And us having sent three ships this month into that very harbor, stripped of all their valuables, just ready to tell all about the *Donnybrook* what robbed 'em? No thank you, mates. I like my neck the length it is. I don't need it stretched."

The crew shuffled and scratched their heads. "Caymans, then?' Mister Bracegirdle called out.

Scarlet nodded and beckoned to the navigator. "Mister Pryce, how many days to the Caymans?"

Mister Pryce was as female as Scarlet herself, though her clothing, a linen shirt, vest and breeches, could have disguised her as a boy if she had not let her long blonde hair fly free. She frowned to herself for only a moment, then replied, "With this wind and these currents, eight days."

The crew looked distraught, and twelve year old William called out, "Can the Shantyman untie his cord?"

The Shantyman stood behind Scarlet on the quarterdeck, and she turned to look at him. He was not an officer, though the crew held him in superstitious awe. His battered, antique clothing was odd in both cut and color, and he kept a dozen mysterious pouches and bags tied about his waist. His job was to sing the sea shanties that kept the ship's work a pleasure, but the magic of the wind was extra.

"The moon's not right," he called down to William, "and I don't loose the winds over a mug o' wine." No one answered.

"So, eight days, and then we have to make a trade." Scarlet shook her head. "Do we at least vote to ration?"

A ragged chorus of "Aye's" and "Might as well's" signaled at least unofficial approval.

"Well," Bracegirdle called, "where can we get in three days?"

Pryce thought, put her hands in her pockets, thought again, and offered, "The mainland. Donnelly boys."

Sunny Jim groaned, "Does anyone think the Donnelly boys own liquor they ain't drunk yet?"

"Does anyone believe the Donnelly boys ain't got liquor?" Scarlet countered. The faces below her brightened. She had them. "Right then. Pryce, plot us a course. Mister Flynn, prepare to work sail. Let's make her fly."

⌘

The Spanish claimed it, but in fact the mainland belonged to no country. Bands of lawless buccaneers roamed through the woods hunting wild hogs, or cutting illegal timber, or paddling out in crude canoes to attack any merchant foolish enough to come close. The Donnelly brothers had built a dozen huts between the beach and the trees, now populated with an assortment of escaped slaves, natives, and runaway bondsmen.

As the longboat rowed toward the beach, Scarlet noticed the inhabitants piling loose sand into a chest-high barricade along the length of the shore. It looked like a crude fort. Not a bad idea; the world was full of trouble. Scarlet had prepared for her trading mission by ordering the *Donnybrook* cleaned, polished and flying a white flag before they sailed into the wide, sheltering cove.

Conner Donnelly came down the beach to meet her, wearing what was probably his best coat, a dirty brocade that stretched tight across his young shoulders. Scarlet smiled in appreciation.

Conner's brothers flanked him on either side. Curly-haired Sean looked nervous, putting his hands in his pockets and taking them out, and Mick was drunk as usual. As they approached, Scarlet could hear Sean whispering, "Conner, I keep tellin' you. We'll fill a chest with rocks and put gold on top of 'em. He'll take the chest, and we're grand."

Conner slapped him on the head. "You think he wouldn't look?"

Scarlet wore her own best coat, embroidered red silk, with a man's shirt, and a woman's brocade skirt pinned up over her sea boots. Burgess and the Shantyman were also in their best. Twenty feet apart, Scarlet bowed and doffed her hat. Conner met her eyes and smiled. Mick leaned forward with a leer.

"That's a fine dress you're wearin', sweetheart. Would ye care to get out of it and come back to my place?"

Conner elbowed him hard, and was punched on the shoulder in return. Mick had a limp, a cutlass scar on his forehead, and a reputation for thinking with his fists. Scarlet laid a hand on her sword. "For God's sake Mick, shut your gob and let a person do business."

"It's our beach. Don't tell me what to do." Mick pulled open his coat to reveal a pistol.

"Ah, Mick," Scarlet smiled, "I wish I had time to send you to the hell where you belong. But I'm speaking with your brother."

Conner turned and punched Mick in the face, hard enough to rock him on his heels. For one second Mick's mouth twisted with rage, but then his hot eyes turned back to Scarlet. "You don't know what you're missin', love."

Scarlet kept her face bland. "Nor do you. Let's keep it that way. Unless Conner's not the one in charge, anymore."

Conner glared at Scarlet and slugged his brother again, shoving Mick right down on the sand, then arranged his face in a smile. "I'm still in charge. Was there somethin' you'd be needing from us?"

Scarlet grinned at him. "We've a hold full of goods and provisions, three tons of the finest dried cod I've ever seen, and gold besides. But we're running low on grog. Have you anything to trade?"

Conner's smile was more natural now. "You come at a good time. A merchant ship hit Ripper Rock not three days ago. We've just finished looting the hulk. I've got rum, French brandy and some banana beer we brew ourselves. Pleasant terms for an honorable woman like yourself. Will you be staying for a while?"

Scarlet winked. Nearly a quarter of the *Donnybrook's* crew were female, and they were warmly welcomed most places. And Conner Donnelly, unlike his brother, was an attractive man. "You know how I favor you, Conner. I'd like nothing better than to spend the night. But let's make a deal first. That way we'll all have something to celebrate."

"A fine idea." Conner was slender, dark and quiet, with the very still face of a young man who'd seen too much, and the expressive eyes of a soul that hoped for the best. "Would you care to come into my office?"

Scarlet nodded to Burgess and the Shantyman, "Come with me."

They followed Conner through a real wooden door set with real metal hinges, into the building, which did have pretensions of being an office. A floor of wooden planks, a lantern suspended from the ceiling, shelving and a desk, all of which looked like they had once been part of a Royal Navy ship. The chairs looked Spanish. An open door showed a much larger room beyond, stacked with barrels and chests. Scarlet and Burgess sat. Conner took his place behind the desk and poured out mugs of beer.

"You've done right well," said Scarlet, smiling. She had always felt that Conner would amount to something.

"We'll be a town someday."

"Old ghosts and ship's bones," the Shantyman intoned, steepling his fingers and looking into the corners of the room. "Some of this is off that new-sunk ship. Have you done a charm to settle the furniture?"

Conner nodded to himself. "We've had the local midwife say a few words. If you know better, I wouldn't take it amiss."

Scarlet smiled. "My da' used to be in your line o' business. We didn't have your fine and fortuitous Ripper Rock. Da' lit watch fires along a bad stretch of coast, so ships would think it were safe passage, and run aground. I know a charm to lay your ghosts. I'll be happy to share, if we reach an accord about the liquor. But business first. How much can you spare, and what do you want?"

Conner rubbed his tongue over his teeth, and looked up into the thatching of the roof, as if the answer might be hiding there. He said, "I can't afford to pay for laying ghosts. But I'll give you eight barrels of rum, and one of the brandy, if your Shantyman will loose three knots of that magic cord he carries."

Burgess raised his eyebrows. Scarlet, whose mind had been on money, and various articles in the *Donny's* hold, paused a moment and let out a long breath. "That would be quite a gale, it would."

"A gale is what I want. A hurricane, if you could promise it wouldn't touch the shore."

Scarlet looked, but the Shantyman's face was as blank as a bucket of milk. "It don't work that way, you only get wind, not direction. What would you be needin' a storm for?"

Conner rose to his feet and began to pace. "We've had a little trouble. Sean has, I mean. A ship came in to trade, and Sean started playing cards with the captain. He's lucky, Sean is, anyone will tell you that, as long as there's no money riding on it. But as soon as he puts down a shilling, all his luck flies out the window. He lost something terrible.

"The feller he lost to wanted to take our whole place here, and sell Sean as a slave to pay the debt. Sean didn't tell me. He told Mick and Mick talked to the fellow. Said he had a deal of his own, going down soon, and he'd hand over twenty full barrels of gunpowder in a month's time, if only the captain would wait."

"That's worth more than a dozen slaves."

"It is. And when the man came back at the end of the month, Mick had the barrels ready for him. Except they weren't full of gunpowder. They were full of sand, with a little powder on top."

Scarlet snorted. "And how did Mick think he'd get away with that?"

Conner shrugged. "Mick and Sean together couldn't explain that to me. Two days ago, a fisherman told us the fellow's coming looking for us, he's less than a week behind, and he's angry." He waved toward the sand wall. "We're trying to build some defenses."

"And you'd be happy to sink the man with my wind." Scarlet turned to the Shantyman. "How many knots in your cord?"

The Shantyman spread his hands, and showed the cord, as silken and free of knots as a bride's hair. "I'm sorry, ma'am. While we were on The Isle of Pines a beautiful young woman promised me anything in the world if I'd bring her father back home. Eyes black as midnight, she had."

Scarlet sighed. "I'd dearly love to help you, but I've no wind to trade." She considered. "That sand-fort you're building ain't much, but I took two extra cannons off an India trader a month or so back. You can have 'em for the liquor. But I want consideration, too. I have salt cod to trade as well, and I'll require two pounds of smoked pork or dried fruit for every pound of cod."

"Done." Conner smiled into her eyes. "You're a good woman. Now, how much gunpowder can you spare?"

Scarlet laughed. "Not twenty barrels! Four casks, let's say. And a dozen balls. You can make more out of stone."

Conner clasped her hand. "I'll set people on it at once. Will you stay for a party tonight? You're making us a handsome trade.'

"We'll be happy to stay for a party." She smiled, looking deep into his eyes,. "But you're providing the rum!"

⌘

Two cannons gave the sand fort a much more impressive appearance, and the crew of the *Donneybrook* dipped their tankards into the barrel of rum at once to toast Scarlet's wise trade.

It was a grand party. One of Conner's people played the fiddle, the Shantyman had the finest voice in all the islands, and four of the natives brought drums. The men and women of Scarlet's crew were pleased by the men and women of the Donnellys, and the Donnellys' crew were pleased with them. A hog roasted over the bonfire, and the dancing went on until everyone had drunk too much to stay on their feet.

Scarlet pulled Conner away to a secluded place behind a ridge of sand.

"It ain't just a place," Conner slurred, holding up a bottle of brandy. "It's safety. Most of these folk never been safe ever in their lives. I want to build a real town, where people c'n be free."

"A grand idea," replied Scarlet, nuzzling along his collarbone.

"He won't take my town from me. And he won't hurt Sean."

Scarlet tugged at his shirt. "Talk later. I've been thinking of you for days." The shirt resisted, so she moved straight to his trouser buttons.

Conner ran a hand along her thigh, through the material of the dress, and began to help with the buttons. They laughed together ant their own clumsy fingers, and when the breeches finally cooperated, Scarlet draped her skirts over him for privacy and stretched out beside him. They looked into each other's eyes for a moment.

"it will be a town," Conner said, "Safe and true. Any you'll help me keep it safe, that and all the folk in it. Ned Doyle won't..."

All Scarlet's relaxed desire left her at once. Almost sober, she sat bolt upright. "Ned Doyle? Red Ned Doyle is the fellow your brothers cheated?"

Conner stared at her, his jaw slack. Scarlet scrambled to her feet, pulling her skirts after her. Ned Doyle? Conner had enraged Ned Doyal? They'd all end up dead!

She looked wildly around for a way to escape. All around, her crew lay passed out on the sand. The *Donnybrook* sat thirty yards out in the cove, empty and at anchor. There was no way she could get away until the tide turned tomorrow. For a while her reeling mind tried to remember when that was, but the calculations kept slipping away. She looked over at Conner, but he was flat on his back, mouth open, snoring.

There was no way to revive her drunken crew. Scarlet collapsed on the sand, sick with worry. She could see no way to save herself or her people.

Finally, her eyes lit on an abandoned brandy bottle, still half full. She scooped it up, raised it to her lips, and sat down to drink her way to oblivion.

⌘

Morning broke clear and very bright, and the glare did nothing to improve Scarlet's temper. She found Conner in his office.

"Ned Doyle. It was Red Ned Doyle, and you didn't tell me."

"Don't be angry. I needed your help." Conner sat, twisting his fingers, stared at a mug of tea in front of him. "You didn't ask."

Sean looked up from his own seat in the corner. "Why's he called 'Red'? His hair's as black as mine."

Scarlet turned to him. "It's for the blood on his hands. Ned Doyle has killed more people than scurvy. And you folk have pissed him off. Now Conner gets me involved."

Conner looked up with those deep, sad eyes. "I'm sorry, Scarlet. I'm not letting him take my brother."

"And I'm not standing in his way. You're a fine man, Conner, and I like seeing you from time to time, but I'm sailing out on the tide. It was a grand party. I'll remember it long after you're dead."

Conner pointed a long finger. "Don't let this place burn. And don't let another Irishman become a slave. You know what our people have been through."

"It'd be a more persuasive argument if Ned Doyle wasn't as Irish as the both of us. I'm getting my own people out. You can take care of yours."

Unconscious pirates lay scattered over the beach. Scarlet walked back and forth, bellowing and kicking the prone forms awake. Her head hurt. For a moment she closed her eyes and thought of Conner in the clutches of Red Ned Doyle, but there was nothing she could do to prevent that. She hadn't stayed alive this long by running a charity fund or a rescue operation.

She couldn't find Pryce. She couldn't find the Shantyman. She began breaking into huts.

An hour later she finally had her crew assembled. Mick stood staring from the door of Conner's office, a bottle in his hand. Scarlet's people looked pale and sick. "There's rum on the *Donnybrook*," she told them roughly. "Let's get in the water."

The longboat was ready on shore, but it would take several trips to get everybody to the ship. Scarlet waited until the last, glaring at Conner. Conner stared at the sand by his feet, and Mick glared back. He was already drunk. Or still drunk, Scarlet wasn't sure.

The longboat was on its third trip, Dark Maire at the tiller, when Scarlet heard the call from her ship, "Sail! Sail on the horizon!"

She took five long steps toward Conner. "You tell me that's anyone on God's earth besides Ned Doyle."

"Shut up!" Mick shouted, reeling forward.

Mick aimed a wild blow at Scarlet's head, but Burgess, good man that he was, managed to get in the way, tripping Mick as much by luck as anything. Sean slugged Burgess in the face. Scarlet aimed a return blow at Sean, but Conner grabbed her fist and held her back. Everyone was shouting. Conner shouted loudest, "Shut up!"

"Aye, shut up and stow it." Scarlet ordered, turning to glare around her. Burgess, Yeboah and the Shantyman were nearby. "Red Ned Doyle is coming over that horizon, and he ain't in the best of moods. What have we got?"

"We've got the *Donnybrook*. We'll just sail away," Burgess offered.

"We don't have the wind for it." Scarlet turned to Conner. "What about the tides? What are the tides doing?"

Conner stared at the beach. "Not much this time of year. It'll turn about noon, but they don't run high. You won't get much help."

"We can tow the *Donny* with the longboat," Scarlet thought out loud.

Conner stepped up and looked at her. "Go ahead. Sail out of here. But take my brothers with you."

She opened her eyes wide in surprise. "What are you saying?"

"Take Mick and Sean and sail on out of here. Ned will land, they'll be gone, and he and I will work something out. Just get my brothers away."

"I'm not takin' your fool brothers." Scarlet looked left and right. "What can we do to increase our chances?"

The Shantyman held up his cord and let it uncoil, showing a single knot. Scarlet stared. "How did you get that?"

"It was a grand party last night. Good for a knot in me cord."

"Then loose it once we're clear of the cove. This land breeze is blowing the wrong way."

"Wait!"

Scarlet rounded on Conner. "What is it now?"

Conner pointed a shaking finger at the Shantyman. "I gave you that knot. My party, my rum, my magic. You owe me. Take my brothers out."

Mick started to shout, and Conner punched him in the face, then turned. Conner's eyes bored into Scarlet, pleading and commanding together.

Scarlet spat on the ground. "The crow's curse on you. All right, I'll take them. But if Ned Doyle kills me for it, I'll haunt you."

"Done." Conner offered his hand, but Scarlet didn't take it. "Well," she snapped a Sean, "My longboat's coming in. Get ready to get on it."

Sean, his face grey, glanced at Conner and stumbled toward the shore. Mick began to argue, yelling that he was no coward and had no plans of going anywhere. Conner got his brother by the ears and stared into his eyes until Mick looked down and nodded. For a moment the two stood, heads together. Then Mick punched Conner affectionately and headed for the water.

Rowing out to the ship, everyone was silent. Sean and Mick kept their heads down. As soon as they touched the *Donny's* side, Scarlet scrambled up the cleats along the ship's side, shouting as she went. "Don't just stand there, you lubbers! The wind's dead against us. Weigh anchor! Get me up a hawser! We need to rig a towline. And clap these two men in irons!"

Sean looked startled, and Mick tried to fight, but they were outnumbered. Scarlet watched Yeboah drag them below with some satisfaction. Blessed Virgin, she might just get away with this.

The *Donnybrook* had no oars, but the longboat did. Scarlet could put six strong sailors in it and tow the much larger ship. It wouldn't be easy, but it could be done. Ned Lynch and the *Cardiff Rose* would sail into the cove, and Scarlet and the *Donnybrook* would row their way out, and with any luck, they'd have no reason to do more than shout a greeting at each other in passing.

"Cap'n?" came Sunny Jim's voice from above. "You need to be up here."

Hell and damnation. Scarlet tucked the skirt of her party clothes up a little higher and clambered up the ratlines.

Sunny Jim handed Scarlet the spyglass as soon as she made the crow's nest. She squinted through it and gasped. The ship coming at them wasn't the *Cardiff Rose*. It was huge. Three times the size of the *Donneybrook*.. The size of a war ship. Had the bloody Royal Navy found the Donnellys?

Scarlet took a deep breath and looked again, noting details. The ship was big, but looked more like a slaver than a frigate. Its deck was raised fore and aft, and it wasn't rigged like the *Falcon*, the only frigate she knew was in the area. The huge vessel had the wind dead astern, and Scarlet couldn't see what flag she flew. The paint on her sides looked recent, and her sails were new and unpatched.

It just didn't make sense. A slave ship had no business coming into an unmarked mainland cove.

Unless they needed water.

Scarlet's mind began to turn from prey to predator. A blundering, lost slave ship, crammed with human cargo just ready to become pirates, short on water, wandering into the Donnelly's cove offered possibilities, and one of those possibilities included Scarlet obtaining a ship that would out-gun Ned. If the *Donnybrook* could get between the slaver and the sea... Slave ships traveled heavily armed, so the trick would be passing, on the towline, without appearing either odd or unfriendly. A broadside from something that size would send them all to a watery grave.

If only she could see the flag! The breeze shifted, and a flash of red showed. Scarlet's mind flew. Red might be the East India Company or Spain. Spain laid claim to the coast, but the Spanish flag was mostly white. Besides, the shape of the thing just didn't lok Spansh. She called down to the main deck. "I think we may have a prize! Load the guns, but toss the covers back over 'em. And run me up an English flag."

Scarlet paced the deck, watching the approaching vessel, calculating wind and water and their own achingly slow progress behind the longboat. She sent all the women down below, instructing them to dress as men. A crew full of females was a sure hint that a vessel was crewed by pirates. When her own turn came, she hastily dug through her sea chest and pulled on breeches, stockings and buckled shoes, throwing her brocade skirt on the floor and wavering for a moment before choosing a worn blue coat. She tucked the tail of her hair under a plain black hat, put pistols in both her pockets, and dashed back on to the deck.

At this rate, they'd meet about a halfway between the mouth of the cove and the shore. Glancing back at the sand fort behind them, Scarlet laughed to herself as the obvious excuse for their hasty departure dawned on her. They were fleeing from a pirate camp!

Scarlet whispered orders. "We'll hold course, they should hang to starboard as we pass. As soon as we've passed her, drop the towline. I want the mainsail run up double-time and we'll go hard-a-starboard and put one shot up her arse. That should take the fight out of 'em. Mr. Bracegirdle, you take the shot. Flynn, run up the black flag as soon as we make the turn. I want all gun crews at the ready. If the one shot don't intimidate 'em, we may have to fight."

In chase or battle, the captain's word was law. The pirates took their places, doing their best to act as if they were merely leaving the harbor. Scarlet wished she could signal to the men in the longboat, but she couldn't risk it.

Closer and closer came the strange ship. Scarlet could pick out people on the deck, see individual faces. The ship wasn't bearing starboard. It was coming right at them. Scarlet shouted for the men in her longboat to get clear, but the strange ship turned at the last moment, luffed her sails, and sat dead in their path. The longboat crew back-paddled and the *Donneybrook* drifted to a halt.

Several familiar faces came out of hiding, and a man in a red shirt called out, "Scarlet, darlin'! How fine to see you! Tie up alongside. We'll have a mug of beer and I'll show you my new ship."

It was Ned Doyle himself.

Scarlet cursed under her breath, smiled and waved. "Ned! I thought you were someone else entire. The ship's grand. Where did you pick her up?"

"Off the coast of Hispaniola." Ned paused to shout down to his own main deck, "Throw the woman a line." Over his head flew the solid red pennant that signaled "no quarter given".

"I'd rather drink beer a little farther from them bleedin' Donnellys," Scarlet offered.

Ned smiled, showing teeth that gleamed white against his bronzed, unshaven face. "And I think we'll be speakin' right here. You looked a lot like you were planning to fire on me, darlin'."

Scarlet laughed. "Of course I was, Ned. I thought you was a slave ship. You'd call me a fool if I let a fat prize like that stumble away." She let her eyes grow cold and hard. "But why were ye' hiding, Ned? You know I'm a pirate. You got no call to be hostile. "

"Maybe I do, and maybe I don't. Come over and we'll talk."

"There'll be a lot of pissed-off folk if you fire on me, Ned."

"Come on aboard, darlin'."

Scarlet looked at his ship. Thirteen guns along a side, to the *Donny*'s five, and a deck that stood eight feet above her own. "I'll come."

Ned led the way to the captain's cabin, a grand room with a full bank of glazed windows across the stern of the ship. The previous occupant had left a huge, red stain on the floor. Ned didn't look moved in, yet. He had to rummage to find whiskey, and the papers still on the desk didn't look like pirate business. Two of his crew followed them in, and the big cabin suddenly felt small. Scarlet kept her breathing even and sipped her drink.

"Good grog, this. It's a grand ship, Ned, but I'd think you'd take more time to get settled in before showing her off. And where's the *Cardiff Rose*? Surely you didn't give her up."

"Nick's in the *Rose*. They're about a day behind, being short on crew. I brought the best lads with me."

Nick Delacroix had been Ned's first mate for the past four years. Before that, it was rumored that he had come from an island where they ate people. In the *Cardiff Rose* he would be almost as dangerous as Ned.

Scarlet kept her tone easy. "I thought you looked short on crew. It's too bad the *Rose* is so far behind. I'd have liked to say hello to Nick."

"What are you doing with the Donnellys'?"

"I'm <u>with</u> nobody." Scarlet kept her face blank. "I come in to trade, and them beggars set me up with bad grog. So I took the first two Donnellys I could lay hands on and I ain't bringing them back until Conner makes it right."

Ned's eyes were hard as flint, but his voice purred. "And what kept you from having it out right then?"

"My own foolishness. I gave them two guns for the wine, and they're all set up on the beach, pointing at me."

"I hear you're smarter than that, Scarlet."

Scarlet kicked a chair around, sat down and took a long drink. "Send somebody over to check. There's seven barrels of vinegar in my hold, and two Donnellys in the brig."

Ned signaled and one of his men left. "The problem is, I've heard a lot about you being sweet on Conner. I think he talked you into giving him them guns and taking his brothers out of my path."

"Conner's got fine eyes and a grand set of shoulders, but I ain't sweet on anyone. And if I'm rescuing those boys, why have I got 'em locked up?"

Ned laughed. "I can think of sixteen reasons why Mick and Sean would be in your brig, and it ain't even noon yet. But my thanks for telling about the guns. Now, what I want you to do is to turn your bloody ship around, sail up to that beach and blow hell out of everything on it. When you're done, I'll come in and do the looting. Don't want to chip the paint on me fine new ship."

With a roar, Scarlet leaped to her feet, threw her mug a Ned and drew a pistol. "Red Ned Doyle, you know me mostly by reputation, so I'll tell you this. The surest way to get on my bad side is to tell me what to do. I take orders from no man. Not from Conner Donnelly and not from you. Do I make myself clear?"

Ned's eyes flashed and he licked his lips. "You're pretty when you're angry, darlin'. Now put that away. I'll go over to your ship and have a look around. If everything's as you say, we'll talk again."

Scarlet kept the weapon pointed at him, but the man behind her grabbed her arm. The gun went off. Ned was already moving and grunted as the shot clipped him, but kept coming. Scarlet wrestled with the seaman, clubbing him on the head with the empty gun. The man sagged to the deck as Ned grabbed Scarlet by the shoulders and lifted her off her feet. She kicked, aiming for the groin, and missed. Ned shook her like a doll.

Her head reeling, Scarlet twisted and bit him on the hand. He turned her and threw her against the bulkhead. Her head struck unyielding oak. Suddenly the whiskey didn't want to stay in her stomach anymore, and last night's pork and brandy came up with it. She clutched the wall, gagging, and glared at Ned.

He stepped up close, avoiding the mess on the deck, and said. "Yes, very pretty. But you've ruined my favorite shirt, and I'll have to get angry with you when I come back. Just wait here, will you darlin'? I've got to reorganize some things on the *Donnybrook*. Warm up the bunk for me, and if you apologize nice, I may let you keep your ship."

Scarlet's mouth tasted of whiskey and bile, and she couldn't think of anything angry enough to say.

Ned dragged his man from the room, and Scarlet heard a key turn in the lock. Blessed Virgin, but she felt sick. She staggered to the desk and washed her mouth out with whiskey, then began to look around. She still had one pistol, but that meant only one shot, and she doubted Ned would be stupid enough to be the first person through the door.

The papers on the desk said the ship was the *Coco Nut,* and that she'd unloaded her slave cargo at Port-au-Prince. Ned must have taken her soon after, floating high and carrying little besides money. The possessions of the former captain were pretty to look at, but didn't run to weapons.

Scarlet groaned and put her head in her hands. A lump was rising on her left temple She needed a plan, but the best thing she could think of was to put the pistol in the bed and shoot Ned when he came to rape her. It was a good plan, except for the fifty or so sadistic pirates who accepted Doyle as their leader.

Jumping out of the window would be wonderful, if she could swim. Or had anyplace to swim to, since Ned now controlled both ships.

"I should have just fired on him when he came alongside," Scarlet murmured to herself, but that wasn't right either. Not only did the *Coco Nut* carry twice as many guns as her own ship, but they were bigger guns. It would have been sheer stupidity to trade broadsides.

Red Ned Doyle didn't deserve this ship. With it, he could tip the power in the Caribbean, terrorize merchants and pirates like. It wouldn't likely be a long reign, but it could be an unpleasant one.

Scarlet could almost hear the moans of the people Ned and his crew had murdered. It didn't have to be like this. One warning shot and most merchants surrendered, gave you everything they had, and sometimes agreed to join your crew. It was a business, like any other. No need to make it bloodier than it had to be.

If only she could raise Ned's victims. The *Coco Nut's* timbers groaned as if in answer. Murdered spirits whispered around the room.

Could she do it? Scarlet knew charms to calm the dead, to release the possessions that former owners clung to after death. Could the spells be reversed? Her eyes darted around the room. She had whiskey, gunpowder, a murdered man's blood, and stood on a slave ship whose tormented cargo had seeped rage and despair into the very hull.

The cabin's lock clicked and the door flew open with a bang. Scarlet leaped to her feet, fumbling for her remaining pistol, only to see the Shantyman shoved roughly into the cabin, and the door slammed shut behind him. She let the gun fall back into her pocket with a nervous laugh. "What're you doing here?"

The Shantyman carried a bundle under one arm, and the whites of his eyes gleamed. "Captain Doyle offered me a new job, and said it'd be good for my health to take it."

"What's he doing over there?"

"He's looking around. Brought the longboat back in. Seems t' think the Donnellys sold us that bad wine. Nobody's corrected him."

"What use could we make with a mite of wind right now?"

"We're drifting toward shore, very slow. A breeze would send us in quicker. But these men would have to be powerful distracted to ground the ship."

"The very thing I have in mind." Scarlet told him her plan, and the Shantyman kissed her on the forehead. "You're the finest captain I've e'er sailed under. And look what I have in me pocket to help." He withdrew a small bag made of black cloth and wrapped three times with a red cord. "I tied this up during that grand battle we had last month. Full of rage it is."

22

Scarlet looked around. She had lived with charms and curses all her life, had cast them and avoided them and told tales of them until far into the night. This was different.

She took a deep breath. The first thing to do, she recalled, was to prepare the space. She took off her shoes and stockings, made signs to the four winds, rubbed her medal of Saint Bridget on its cord around her neck, and slowly removed the powder cartridge from her pistol. She spread gunpowder over the blood on the deck, followed it with a generous splash of whiskey, and then opened the bag of anger.

She could feel a chill come upon the hot Caribbean air. For a moment she paused, fear clawing at her throat, not sure what she was calling up. The ghosts in the room moaned for vengeance, cried out in despair. Scarlet had felt plenty of rage and despair in her own life. She took a deep breath, concentrated on the memory of helplessness growing into rage, held her body and mind perfectly still, and opened her heart to the creatures swirling around her.

The air in the cabin went suddenly frigid. Scarlet sensed a presence behind her, but was afraid to look. The Shantyman's face went dead white, and he began to sweat. All around them, the ship made restless noises. Timbers creaked and groaned as if a storm had risen, and the bright Caribbean sun seemed to dim.

Human noises went quiet. Scarlet could imagine every man aboard suddenly stopping work and looking around in unease. The rush of water under the hull seemed loud.

"Let's go home," she whispered to the Shantyman, and he nodded in silence. Scarlet picked up a heavy chair and smashed it against the paneled wooden door. The latch shattered and she walked out, still in her bare feet, the Shantyman following.

Faces of the dead rose in her mind. Her mother's face, in its shroud. The first drowned man she'd ever seen. A young sailor, his head shattered by a falling spar. The first man she'd ever killed. A dead child. The corpse of a slave. Her father as she'd sewn the canvas over his face before burying him at sea.

She felt her way along the passage, seeing only the dead, feeling the Shantyman's warm hand clutching at the tail of her coat as they stumbled along.

A living voice began to moan. Another wept. Then the screaming started.

By touch alone she found her way to the companionway and up the ladder. As she staggered across the deck she could hear men flinging themselves into the sea.

At last the voices of her own crew cut through the other sounds. She found her way toward them, and tumbled over the rail and onto the *Donneybrook*'s precious deck.

The sun was bright again, and the air warm. Then the Shantyman fell on top of her.

Scarlet crawled to her feet with a groan. "Cut the lines. Cut all lines to that ship. Hoist the sail, get ready for wind."

Red Ned stood on the deck, holding a battered Sean Donnelly by the hair. His other hand carried a pistol. "What the shite is going on?"

"Your new ship don't like you anymore." Behind Scarlet, Ned's sailors wept, collapsed, clawed at their own eyes. The ship shivered and groaned.

"Then I'll have to take yours." Three of his men stood nearby, also armed, Mick's blood-covered body at their feet. Ned spoke to them. "Bring that cow over here."

Scarlet had put the second pistol back in her pocket. She pulled it now and cocked it in one smooth motion, giving no hint that it held no powder. "The longboat's all you get. Lower it, get on it, and get out of here."

Three pistols were pointed at her, but the men with Ned kept glancing at their comrades on the other ship. The whites of their eyes gleamed, and they were sweating despite the breeze.

Breeze. Scarlet's eyes darted back to the Shantyman, and the cord, free of knots, that lay beside him.

Ned roared and stepped forward, dragging Sean, his pistol aimed at Scarlet's head. Sean croaked, "Help me!" And Mick Donnelly came off the deck.

He was so beaten that he hardly looked human, but somehow he had managed to get his legs under him, and he plowed into Ned like a bull, knocking him over. The pistol went off. Scarlet didn't feel anything strike her, so she turned her own pistol butt-first and pegged Ned Doyle right between the eyes.

His men threw down their guns.

The two ships were drifting. Scarlet could see figures on shore crowded around the guns. "Hoist the damn sail," she shouted. "We have wind. Move! We need to get clear of that ship!" The *Donny's* sails filled, and as she made way Scarlet felt the rudder catch, and they bore away to starboard, the blue water slipping past her hull and the *Coco Nut* falling away behind them.

"You want us to make land?" called Pryce from the quarterdeck.

"Might as well. We've got Donnellys to deliver. And I think Ned's still alive, we'll have to think of something to do with him."

Bracegirdle called out. "Should we fire on Ned's ship?"

Scarlet turned to look. The chaos on the *Coco Nut* seemed to have abated somewhat, but the ship was still in no state to defend herself. She looked back to shore, saw the puff of smoke from the first gun, and heard the boom less than a second later. "Don't do it," she said. "Ned's still a pirate, and it's still against the Code. Conner will take care of the matter for us. It's his fight."

She walked over to the Donnellys. Sean sat on the deck, head cradling his head, and Mick lay on his back, looking up at the sky with the one eye he could still open. "I'm taking you back to your brother," she told them. "In the meantime, would you like a mug rum for the pain?"

25

Mick nodded faintly. Sean said, "Sure," then smiled. "You're coming back? Does that mean we can have another party tonight? Maybe we can play some cards."

Settling Accounts

"Ship ahoy! Six points off the starboard bow!"

Scarlet stood near the rail, squinting. She saw nothing, of course, not having the elevation of the lookout on the mast head. Nevertheless, she heaved a sigh of relief. It was good to be away from Ned Doyle. And even good to get away from Conner Donnelly, grand shoulders or not.

Back to good, honest pirating.

The *Donnybrook* cut through the water at nearly ten knots, running at her best point of sail, her great mainsail belled out drumtight by the steady trade wind. Her crew spent a few minutes doing what her captain had done, looking for the prey. Then different activities broke out, as folk pulled out pistols and cutlasses, and began general preparations for an attack.

Many members of the crew had special raiding clothes, bits of old armor, or pieces of stolen finery that proclaimed their success in former attacks. The women let down their hair. Scarlet, who had no knack for putting her hair up like a lady, had realized long ago that nothing frightened a gentleman more than a screaming woman with her hair flying wild and a weapon in hand.

All the while Sunny Jim called down reports. "Looks to be a good-sized barque!"

"Something funny about her."

"Sails are luffing. She's dead in the water."

By this time the ship had come over the horizon, and Scarlet raised her glass to see. A dead ship was no good thing. For a vessel to be so untended that it had lost its wind and was rolling with the sea-swells, something dreadful must be wrong.

A short list ran through her mind as she searched the distant vessel for evidence. The reason for the abandonment…

"Do you think its plague?' Sunny Jim asked, a quaver in his voice.

The crew stirred nervously, and Scarlet cursed under her breath. Trust Sunny Jim to cut straight to the worst possible answer. She forced herself to laugh out loud in response, and shouted back so that everyone could hear. "More like they're lost and perishing from thirst! Be glad, they will, for us to rescue their sorry hides, and willing to give up all their treasure in payment!"

The pirates laughed in return, and began to elbow each other, speculating what goods the ship might hold. Scarlet nodded to herself and climbed up the ratlines for a better view.

Yes, the boat was drifting. No, there was no sign of plague. Figures moved briskly around on her deck, though their movements were strangely random, not the purposeful activities of men preparing to set sail. Scarlet watched them a while, and began to develop an idea, though she kept it to herself for the time being.

The *Donnybrook* did not raise her black flag, but instead came up like any curious ship seeing such a strange sight. Scarlet hailed the strangers herself, making a trumpet of her hands and calling out, "Ahoy! Unknown ship! Are you in need of assistance?"

A flurry of activity on the strange ship. Scarlet noted that no one on board was wearing an officer's coat or hat. And instead of calling over in a friendly fashion, the men on the vessel huddled together deliberating before one ragged fellow seemed to shout the others down and returned the hail.

"Stay away! There is sickness on board!"

"They ain't sick!" Scarlet said to her crew, before Sunny Jim could make his opinion known. "They're a-trying to fend us off."

"What do we do, Cap'n?" asked Pryce, from the wheel.

The two ships were closing fast. Scarlet replied, "Hold steady!" Then she bellowed back across the water, "Sorry! We can't hear you!" A standard ploy.

"Should we raise the black flag?" asked Flynn.

"We will not." Scarlet stood chewing on her lower lip. "No need to spook 'em. There is something dreadful wrong on that ship, but it's nothing to do with sickness."

Despite repeated efforts by the others to fend them off, the *Donny* came in until she was close enough that a biscuit could be tossed from one vessel to the other.

At this point the same young man who had hailed them pulled a pistol from his breeches and pointed it at Scarlet . "Damn you, I told you to keep away!"

Scarlet disregarded the gun. She had seen the eyes of too many folk aimed at killing, and that was not the expression on this man's face at all. Instead she called back, "Good afternoon to you, young fellow. Is there, by any chance, a mutiny in progress?"

His expression hardened, and his face went dead white.

"Flynn," Scarlet called over her shoulder. "You may run up the Black now."

The *Donnybrook*'s colors, an unadorned black flag, ran up the lines and burst free at the top of the main mast. The fellow on the other ship followed it with his eyes, then looked back to Scarlet. The arm holding the pistol wavered and fell to his side.

"Permission to come aboard?" Scarlet called.

The young man looked at the flag again. "All right," he said. "But only the captain."

"That would be me."

The *Donny*'s crew bound the two ships together, and Scarlet leaped over.

She introduced herself and held out her hand, and after a moment the young man took it. "Moses Hooper," he said. "I'm..." he looked to the frightened, ragged, scrawny mass of sailors behind him. "I'm the acting captain of the *Swan*."

"A lovely name for a lovely craft," Scarlet replied, thought the *Swan* was in no way out of the ordinary. "And why would you be acting captain, instead of captain right and proper, having took the ship?"

The crowd on the deck began to murmur and stir, and Moses shouted at them to be quiet. "Well... There's a number of things we ain't worked out yet."

Scarlet frowned. She'd heard tales of many a mutiny, and planning was always a key part of the successful ones. And yet here was Mister Hooper, nominally in charge of a mutinous crew, and with no idea what he was even in charge of. She began with a couple of business-like questions.

"Where are the officers?"

Hooper swallowed. "Locked in the Captain's cabin."

"Which ones?"

"Captain Clark, Mullett, the mate, and Jacobs." He paused and looked at her. "Do y'mean to rob us now?"

"Well, that depends as well. What plan do you have?"

Just then another man broke in. "I want to go back to Shelmeston!"

Hooper turned on him in a rage. "Well, you ain't going back to Shelmeston, is you? We've took the ship from her rightful captain, and we'll hang if they find out."

Another voice raised. "We could push 'em over. Into the sea, and say they drownded..."

Not a strong-minded group of mutineers. Scarlet chewed on her lip and considered. "What happened?"

The crew stopped its complaining, and Hooper's fists clenched. "He hit the old man."

Scarlet blinked. She had heard of quite a number of reasons to mutiny... Brutal officers, inhuman workloads, a ship in a dangerous state of disrepair. But she had never yet heard of an entire crew rising up because of one blow to one man. Carefully, she asked, "Is the old man still alive?"

Wordlessly, Hooper led her to the lee side of the deck. Under an improvised awning lay a very old man. His few wisps of hair were pure white, as was the stubble that covered his chin. He was lean, dried, weathered like very old leather, with odd discolored spots on his head, cheeks and forearms. Scarlet had seen some like him, but not many. Every line of his body, every hair on his head spoke of extreme age.

His head had been struck and bloodied by some heavy object. His only movement was the slow rise and fall of his boney sides. His eyes were closed.

Scarlet took a deep breath. "Tell."

"Well... " Hooper took a deep breath, then let it out again. "He's... He's old. He knows everything. When our mangy old mainsail split in a blow, he knew how to keep us on course until we could get it fixed. When we run out of water he knew an island that weren't even on the charts. He fixed Billy's arm, and it's good as new..."

"But Clark didn't like 'im!" someone broke in. "Thought 'e weren't pulling 'is weight!"

"Bastard!"

"Clark don't know shit..."

The angry sounds rose, and Scarlet raised her own voice to be heard over them. "We have a woman on my ship who's a healer. Let her come over and look at this man. She may be able to save him."

At the words "save him" the crowd went silent.

31

"Bring her over," Hooper said.

Scarlet called for Branna, and the former midwife came over, with a basket full of herbs and her own great store of dignity, so that the men of the *Swan* instinctively bowed down before her. Branna knelt on the deck and called for hot water and someone went off to the galley to get some.

Scarlet drew Hooper aside. "What happens if he dies?"

"They'll likely raise up and kill Clark."

Scarlet looked pointedly at Hooper's rags and too-thin limbs. "You want him dead?"

Hooper looked at the deck. "I don't rightly want anyone dead." He glanced at Branna. "Are you all women, over there?"

Scarlet shook her head. "Not quite half. The ship's mine... Or was before we turned pirate."

Hooper watched Branna work over the old man for a while. "How... How did..."

Scarlet grinned. "It were my ship, but merchants don't want to deal with a woman. Kept thinking they could cheat me, cheat the crew. I finally had enough. Pulled a gun on a feller. The crew was sick of it, too, so they went with me. We're Irish, most of us, so no one likes us anyway."

"So what happened with the boat?"

"Pirates, real pirates, hold all in common. So the boat was mine, but now everyone on her holds an equal share. Well, not quite equal. I get two share, being captain, and the officers get one-and-a-half. But it comes out pretty even. Plunder – whatever we rob, or take, or find, gets divvied out the same way." She paused to look at him. "You might want to take note, seeing as you'll likely become pirates yourselves, if you choose to live."

"What do you mean, if we choose to live?"

"Well, you could go back to Shelmeston. Hope it works out. It likely won't. Or you could try throwing the bodies overboard, like the man said. But both of them ideas rely on a mob of folk keeping their stories straight for ten years or more…"

Hooper laughed. "That won't happen."

"It never does."

An argument broke out between several of the sailors; shouting, waving fists. Hooper walked away and got in the middle of it.

Members of the *Donnybrook*'s crew began to cross between the ships. Even Burgess, stiff in his businessman's coat, managed to climb across the gap. Scarlet moved forward to shoo them away. But the pirates were neither chasing nor running not fighting, and so Scarlet could do little besides offer advice. "Get the hell off of here" she told them. "These fellers need time to think."

The *Swan*'s sailors had barely started to sort out whatever they were arguing about when Hooper saw the pirates crowding aboard his ship and pulled his pistol.

Scarlet got between him and her crew. "Now, just calm down. Nobody is going to do nobody harm."

"The hell we won't," replied Bracegirdle, the *Donny*'s Gunnery Master. "We come here to rob these folk, did we not? What's holding up the action?"

Scarlet made soothing gestures with her hands, as if trying to calm a restive cow. "Give the fellow a minute. This crew's trying to decide if they'll turn pirate."

"Well, they had better make up their minds." Other members of the *Donny*'s crew joined in.

Hooper waved the pistol. "Shut your bleeding mouths!"

"Shhhhh." Scarlet took a few steps to port. The pirates moved into the space she had vacated, and Hooper stepped back, pushing his people behind him, so all together the crowd formed a rough circle. "Hooper!" Scarlet said in a carrying sort of voice. "I speak with some authority, having been on the account for near five years. Will you hear me?"

Hooper nodded, but the *Swan*'s men behind him muttered and cursed.

"And you, good sailors. May I speak with you? It's only your good I have at heart, and there's no reason you need to mind my words after they've come out of my mouth."

The muttering died down a little, but did not quiet entirely. Scarlet's eyes swept around the circle. Her own folk were restless. They had expected plunder, not negotiations. Scarlet kept her voice cheerful.

"It's three choices you have, the way I figure." She met eyes, first Hooper, then the men behind him. "You can let the Captain go, and take your beatings for what you done, and hope you ain't hanged in the next port. There ain't much chance of that. The powers that be are mad as hell they can't catch the true pirates in these waters. They'll like take it out on you, and you'll swing."

"Or you can jump ship, leave the vessel to them it belongs to by law, and take your chances on the nearest island. Plenty as has done it is alive today, provided they have a little luck and can hunt and build shelter.

"Or you can go on the account. It's not any nevermind of mine if you turn pirate. But it's a grand life, I'll tell you. And it bodes best for your old man, for he stands to live best if you keep the ship under him."

"Ain't you going to rob us?" asked one of Hooper's men.

"We might." Beside Scarlet, Bracegirdle stepped forward and opened his mouth. Scarlet raised her voice and talked over him. "That we will do. Provided you flee the ship or go back to your masters.

At the word "masters" Hooper clenched his fists.

The fellow who wanted to go back to Shelmeston made a whining noise and said to those around him, "Let them do it. Let them kill the captain, and we all can go free."

Bracegirdle pulled a pistol out of his sash, and Scarlet slapped it from his hand. "We'll do no killing on another's account. You lot want the men dead, do it yourselves."

Sunny Jim, from Scarlet's side, called out, "Let's just rob these lubbers and go!"

At that, everyone began shouting. The two sides surged together. Sunny Jim tackled one of the *Swan*s. Another of the *Swan*'s men threw a punch at Pryce, who dodged and slugged him back. Scarlet saw no way to get it stopped, and backed off, trying to get between the brawl and the *Donnybrook,* for pirates were beginning to swarm over, and she did not want a full-scale battle on her hands.

A lone pistol-shot banged out, and folk went suddenly still. Everyone paused for a moment in surprise.

Branna stood just outside the shade of the awning, holding a pistol clumsily in both hands. Smoke hung about the barrel for a moment, and then the light breeze tore it to shreds and carried it away. The healer's eyes were hard.

'Have none of you no respect at all?" she asked, her voice shaking with rage. "There's a man dying here. A good man from the look of it. Will you give him no peace?

Hooper went white and turned to go to the old man's side. His shipmate went with him, and Scarlet held back her own people. Bracegirdle was swearing under his breath.

"It's respectful you'll be," Scarlet told him firmly. "There's a sailor dying, and the same will happen to you one day."

The gunner scratched at the deck with his hobnailed shoe. "Should have robbed 'em and gone on."

Scarlet glared. "As long as we're robbing, the captain's in charge. That means me. And if we ain't robbing, then we'll act like civilized folk."

The *Swan*s gathered around the still form, heads bowed. Many had their hands clasped, as if in prayer. Hooper knelt on the deck, and Branna also went to her knees, her skirts spreading around her, and began wiping the old man's head with a damp cloth. At the sight of the solemn group, the *Donnybrooks* grew quiet.

Scarlet could hear the old man's labored breathing over the lapping of the waves. Then the sound of it grew more shallow, faster. Finally she lost it in the shipboard noises. The crowd around the body bent their heads more deeply but did not move. Finally she head a groan… A last groan, Scarlet knew the sound well. Then there was silence.

But only for a minute. First the *Swans* began to stir and swear, and then Hooper climbed to his feet and stormed off toward the hatchway, his face like a thundercloud.

He came up a few minutes later, driving before him three men in linen coats. Clark was easy to pick out. He only looked outraged. The other two looked frightened, at least.

Hooper grabbed Clark by the sleeve and dragged him to where the old man's body lay on the deck. By this time Branna had covered the man's face, but Hooper ripped the cloth off and shoved Clark toward the body. "There you bastard!" Hooper shouted, "Look what you've done?"

The captain, a corpulent, red-faced man, whose bulk stood in stark contrast to his scrawny sailors, stared at the body and made a dismissive sound through his teeth.

Hooper's eyes were hard. "You killed him, you murdered him, you bastard!"

Clark sniffed. "I did no such thing. A man has been chastised for not doing his duty." He raised his eyes and swept the deck. "It's what you'll all get, if you don't stop this nonsense immediately. I have treated you like my own children, and this is the thanks I get!"

"Makes you right sorry to imagine the state of his household," Scarlet muttered. Bracegirdle nodded his agreement.

Clark glared at the men. "Now, stop this footling around. We need to be in Saint Thomas in four days, and we're behind schedule. Put that piece of trash into the water, and get back to your work, and we'll hear no more about it."

He seemed to feel that this was a perfectly reasonable response to the events of the day, and stood looking about him, as if he expected to be obeyed. Beside him, the mate and Jacobs – probably the bos'un – showed a much more healthy state of fear. Clark, however glared around, wanting for the men to move.

"Put the trash over the side?" asked Hooper in a low, dangerous voice.

"And lets' get back to work," Clark replied.

"I'll put the trash over!" Hooper raised the butt of his pistol and came at his commander. Only then did Clark seem to realize his danger. He threw up an arm and fell back, pure terror on his face.

"I'll put out the bloody trash!" Hopper brought the pistol-butt down, a hard crack on Clark's head that rang in the quiet. Clark shrieked. The pistol came down again, and again and again. When Clark fell, Hooper followed him down, pounding with the wooden butt of the gun, over and over until the former captain's head was a bloody pulp.

Hopper stood. His own crew stared at him in shock.

"Put the trash over the side," Hooper ordered, and four of his men rushed to obey him.

Scarlet stepped forward. "There you go, Captain Hooper."

He looked into her eyes and nodded.

Scarlet gestured to Mullett and Jacobs. "Either of these folk your navigator?"

The new captain nodded to Mullett. "That one."

Scarlet spoke, both to the mutineers and to Mullett. "All right then. Don't harm the man unless he offers you harm himself. And you, Mullett. Understand then that if you serve these men, you're just as much a pirate as they. You'll hang just as quick."

"Bu… But I have no choice!"

Scarlet smiled pleasantly. "Of course you do. You may let them kill you now, and die an honest man."

His eyes told her what she knew they would. Life was too precious to throw away for the sake of honor.

Hooper looked uncertain. "What do we do next? Where do we go?"

Scarlet thought. "Well, if might be a good thing if you broke open the officer's stores and had something to eat. A wake for the old man, like."

"And then?"

"Try Nassau port. It's the heart of the pirate empire in the New World. You can sell the ship, or her cargo, and meet some of the boys. 25.0600 degrees north, 77.3450 degrees west. We're headed there ourselves, in a bit. You'll need to beat into the wind, but it'll be a sight easier if everyone has a full belly.

"Come on," she said to her crew. "Back to the ship. These folk have decided, and we don't rob our own."

The fellow who wanted to go back to Shelmeston shrieked out, "I done nothing! Hooper killed him, I done nothing!"

Scarlet paused and looked over her shoulder. "You let it happen, right along with 'im." Then she smiled and winked. "Give us a try, luv. You may not mind being a pirate after all."

The Governor

The place was New Providence town and Nassau Port, the island of pirates. No nation claimed it, or had for nearly five years. To fill the gap of leadership, pirates had moved in and made the place their home. Now the residents were free from more casual raiders, and the boldest of merchant captains came in to make astounding profits, bringing powder and shot and rum to the most dangerous men on earth.

On the surface it looked no different from any other Caribbean city. Sweating men pushed barrows down the street, and a girl leading a cow called, "Milk! Fresh milk here!" The humid air hung heavy with the scent of over-ripe bananas. The old Governor's Palace stood undamaged by warfare. It was placed back from the street, a serious-looking English construction, but its stern stone façade was brightened by tropical flowers.

Scarlet shifted the small, heavy chest on her left hip as she approached the building. Henry Avery, who had moved in two years past, ans was called the pirate king, had summoned her, and she didn't know why. Her only comfort was the weight of the sword hanging from her belt.

She knocked, uneasily, gave her name and was escorted in by a clerk in a tan linen suit, the front resplendent in pewter buttons.

Scarlet eyed the walls, all smooth plaster and fine paintings, and the windows, glazed and hung with silk drapes. After all the trouble that the Island of Nassau had seen, this place had come through in impressively fine shape. The homes of the rich usually did. She felt rough and ill-bred, but the sword was still at her hip.

The clerk knocked on an elaborate set of double doors and called in, "Miss Scarlet MacGrath!"

"*Captain* MacGrath," Scarlet growled.

"Captain. I'm sorry. Captain."

A muffled voice called from inside the room, and Scarlet entered, careful to go right-foot-first. A pirate needed all the luck she could get.

Afternoon sun filled the room, and cast a golden halo around the wide mahogany desk which stood facing the door. Behind it sat a man of impressive height and more impressive bulk, dominating the space by sheer size. His clothing, an embroidered coat and blindingly white shirt, matched the room, but his hands, sorting the papers before him, were scarred. It could be no one but Avery. His shaved head gleamed in the sunlight, and a curled wig sat on the desk beside him, like some exotic pet.

Scarlet bowed, formally, sweeping off her hat.

"Come in, come in." The man stood, showing a sagging shape, still more chest than belly, and waved a hand, indicating a spindly, ornamented chair. "So you're MacGrath. Sit. You want rum, girl?"

From another man, Scarlet might have taken offense at being called "girl", but now she held her tongue. Avery was well old enough to be her father. She put the chest on the edge of the great desk and perched carefully on the chair.

"What's this?" His right hand, decorated with rings, yet missing the tip of the index finger, indicated the chest.

"A present from the officers and crew of the *Donnybrook*." There had been a discussion, and a vote. Better to be careful when dealing with a man like Avery.

Avery snared the chest and turned it toward him, and Scarlet watched his face as he opened the lid. Inside were two dozen neat stacks of gold coins, with necklaces thrown on top for show. The jewelry had been her idea. Colored gems looked flashy, but you could never fence the stuff for what it was probably worth.

Avery smiled in pleasure, and Scarlet relaxed a little. Even without gems, the chest was worth enough to crew a merchant sloop for a year.

Scarlet accepted a glass of very fine rum, and waited expectantly while Avery settled himself and drank. He pursed his lips and studied her, sharp eyes darting over her face and form. Suddenly he barked out a question. "D'you accept me as Governor of Nassau?"

She blinked. "Why wouldn't you be?"

"I want clarity. I don't claim the title of king, though folk may call me that. You accept me as Governor of Nassau. D'you also accept me as *your* governor?"

Scarlet shifted uneasily in her chair. "Meanin' no disrespect, sir. I do understand that it's your great warship out in the harbor, and your fort pointin' all them guns down at the rest of us. You took this port and held it, and you're the most successful pirate that's ever lived. But no man is in charge of me or mine. I want no trouble. That's just the way it is."

"Yet you came when I asked."

"Because you asked, sir, and asked right nice." She could still feel of the creamy paper of the note under her fingers.

"Then I'll ask nicely again. Will you please tell me what the devil is this business between Red Ned Doyle and the Donnellys? Ned's been going through this port trying to start a war."

"I didn't see all of it, though I heard a great deal of shouting."

"Did Conner Donnelly fire on Ned?"

"He did. Ned was coming up the harbor to fire on him."

"How d'you know?"

Scarlet could hear the ire in her own voice. "Because Ned tried to get me in on it. I told him it was against the Code, and I wouldn't."

"Then what happened?"

"Me and Ned had a disagreement."

Avery cocked an eyebrow, and Scarlet crossed her arms over her breasts. She did not want to even hint that being female had cost her in her fight with Ned Doyle. It was hard enough to be a captain and a woman at the same time.

But Avery's eyes bored into her, and didn't look away, so she lowered her eyes and spoke. "Me and Ned, and one of Ned's men had a fistfight, and the two of them together managed to knock me on the head. So I come back later and knocked Ned on the head. I figure we're even."

"What about the other man?

"I'd already knocked him on the head."

"Ned claims you bewitched him."

Scarlet looked up sharply. "That's been every man's claim since Adam. Ned Doyle had picked up a slaver, and the ship was haunted." She shuddered, despite herself. "Things… came out of the decking. Men's sins come to find them. Ned's a great sinner, and his crew with him."

"Some people want me to do something about Ned. Some want me to do something about the Donnellys."

"The Donnellys ain't in your port. If Ned still is, you ought to invite him onto the *Fancy* for dinner. Drop a hint or two. All them guns – it's forty-six, ain't it? - are like to make an impression. Ned's no fool."

"A fine idea, girl," Avery nodded to himself. "Now, I'll ask you one more thing. Even though I don't govern you, will you do me a favor?"

"It depends on what the favor is, and what I'll be getting out of it."

Avery threw his head back and laughed. "Oh, MacGrath, you're a pirate true! I want you to take this letter," he waved another piece of the creamy writing paper, "to Lord Everand Wellford, the Governor of Tortuga Island. Deliver it personal, and wait for a reply. Influence the reply to be yes, if you can. Do you think you can do that?"

"Maybe, maybe not. What's in the letter?"

"A request for the man to turn pirate. I'll send along a gift, and explain to him what he can get out of it. Nassau Port is the heart of what could be a Pirate Empire. But we're too isolated. If we were in alliance with Tortuga, we'd be far more than twice as strong. Governor Wellford already ignores many things that go on in his port city, and he takes money from people he shouldn't, rich merchants mostly. I'm going to send him a great deal more money, and a proposition."

"Why not go yourself in the *Fancy*?"

"The *Fancy* is a grand ship, and she throws more iron than any in the islands. But I need her here, every day, to protect the port and deal with the like of Red Ned Doyle."

"Why me?"

"You've a good reliable ship and folk call you honest. I'm sending you off with five hundred pounds worth of gold. I want it to get there. I don't think you'll steal from your own."

"And what do we get out of it?"

"Name what you want."

Scarlet ticked off items on her fingers. "A new mainsail for the *Donnybrook*, three spars, four hundred fathoms of rope, a new rudder-chain, and a fresh coat of paint. A proper one, green and gold."

"You drive a hard bargain, Madame."

"I do indeed."

⌘

Back on the *Donnybrook,* Scarlet cast off her shoes and her stifling velvet coat, and called the crew to council. The pirates gathered in, finding seats on equipment lockers, cannons and piles of rope. She began by reciting Avery's offer.

"That's all the things we'd come to Nassau to bargain for." Burgess peered over his spectacles in astonishment.

"It is. And this is the only port in the world that'd slap a coat of paint on a pirate ship."

The crew held council on deck, at dusk. Scarlet spread her bare toes and enjoyed the evening breeze. She told them of what Avery had asked, and the talk went round for a while.

"I don't quite understand this," said Pryce. "I've heard Avery called the king of the pirates, though he's got no royal blood that anybody knows, but now you call him 'governor' as if some crown had set him up to keep order in the place."

"Avery set himself up to rule," Scarlet replied. "And he don't order, he asks. Means a sight, that does."

McNamara, the ship's carpenter chimed in. "All the real kings wanted it, but Avery got it, and he holds it. Fixed up the fort, made peace wt the natives. It's ours."

"That's right," Scarlet leaned forward. "The *Fancy* chases off any warships as want to start trouble. The port belongs to the pirates."

Burgess nodded. "Open port to any merchant who wants to trade with us."

"And now…" Scarlet looked seriously into the faces. "He wants us to run an errand for him. Maybe set up another free port. Can you imagine what that will mean?"

Pryce frowned. "So you think we should do as he asks?"

Scarlet looked from face to face. "I do."

William cleared his throat and spoke. "Will it be safe, d'you think?"

"Oh, no, young William." The Shantyman's voice was deep in the quiet. "It won't be safe. The world ain't a safe place to be in. But Tortuga's governor is half pirate already."

"It'd be a pleasure to fly before the wind, all the way to Tortuga," Pryce said wistfully, running a hand through her blonde hair.

"And de man Henry Avery, he would owe us a favor," added Mister Yeboah.

"Then we're for it?" asked Scarlet.

"Before we go," asked Sunny Jim, "Tell us about that necklace what you're wearin'."

Scarlet's hand went to her throat, where a red gem the size of her thumbnail dangled, surrounded by pearls, strung on a chain of heavy gold.

"Did Henry Avery give you that?"

"He did. Picked it out of a fine box in the governor's office, and told me to wear it round my neck 'til the letter was in Wellford's hand."

"And why is that?"

"D'you think he means to court you?" asked William.

"Do you think," asked the Shantyman, leaning close to Scarlet's ear, "That he's offering Wellford something very precious, that is not his to trade?"

"I don't think so," Scarlet replied. "He told me that he wants the Governor of Tortuga to know that the Governor of Nassau has servants who wear rubies."

⌘

The Caribbean sun shown down on a sparkling sea, and the trade winds blew steady, driving the *Donnybrook* before it, her bow leaping over the swells and falling back, throwing up spray in glittering rainbows. Pryce stood at the wheel, while below, in the great aft cabin, Mr. Burgess, in his severe brown coat, tried to teach Scarlet manners.

They glared at each other over the table. "You're no seaman, Mister Burgess," Scarlet growled.

"You are quite right in that. But I at least know how to eat with a fork."

Scarlet sighed. Burgess had never looked or acted like a pirate. He looked like someone who ate with a fork. "And since when is my belt-knife not good enough?"

"When you're in the company of an English lord that you're trying to persuade to do something."

"Bloody English."

"You'd best be careful, or I'll lose my temper and leave you to Pryce for lessons. She's the only one on this beast of a ship that knows how to eat like something besides a barbarian." Burgess' small mouth drew down and he spat on the deck. "Now, it's going to be on the left side of the plate, with the napkin…"

On the second day, Pryce came up from the hold with a dress and pearl earrings. "For your meeting with the Governor."

"Since when is my coat and skirt not good enough?"

"Since you're trying to win a governor's favor." Pryce rolled her eyes and grinned, holding the fine silk dress in front of her own shirt, vest and breeches. "Come on, you're Irish. Use your charms to support Avery in his damn rebellion."

"Very well."

Burgess huffed. "Why are you so set on the coat?"

"Pockets, Burgess. They're wonderful for holding pistols."

Pryce sighed. "You've got to remember, Tortuga is at least supposedly under control of the Crown. What is going on there is mostly the work of corrupt merchants. There's even been talk of trying to clean it up."

Scarlet shrugged. "That's been goin' on for years."

"Which means it could happen," Burgess replied. "And we mean to walk up to the front door of the Governor's Palace and knock. He's not a pirate yet."

"Five hundred pounds in gold should be a lot more persuasive than me in a dress."

Pryce only frowned, but Burgess answered. "Virgin help us that it should be so."

⌘

Low mountains ringed Tortuga's harbor. No one had bothered to fortify them, but the old Spanish fort dominated the harbor, its looming shape and dark stones casting a shadow over the taverns and whorehouses below. Most of the mooring and the larger buildings were of Spanish construction as well, but newer buildings, in the English style were beginning to rise. The port bustled with ships of many nations. Pryce let a pair of rowboats tow them into a berth, and tossed down a penny. All around sailors toiled, and tradesmen and doxies called their wares. The air smelled of wood smoke, fish and chamber pots.

Scarlet and Burgess were already dressed, and set off on their mission at once. "Pryce says this ain't even the full rig," Scarlet muttered to Burgess as she tried to settle the spreading folds of her dress in the rented carriage. "How does a person move?"

"Carefully. Is my neck cloth straight?" Burgess looked nervously around. "The chest is secured to the back of the coach. We should be all right going in. Here, I brought you these."

Scarlet looked. "Gloves? Am I not covered up enough already?"

"Your hands are stained with tar."

Scarlet put the gloves on, and bore the jouncing ride to the Governor's Palace with only the slightest wriggling against her dress. To distract herself, she looked out at the harbor. "Something tall coming in. Maybe an Indiaman. I can't see her colors from here."

"Don't daydream about prizes. We're trying to be diplomats."

So she turned her head the other way, and watched the town sliding past, first the rough buildings around the dock, then more respectable establishments, and finally, as they moved up into the hills, the spreading, manicured homes of the rich. Watching a beggar being roughly turned away from a grand house Scarlet murmured to Burgess, "Pryce's idea to wear a grand dress weren't so bad. If only I could sit back…"

The driver pulled up, finally, in front of the grandest house that they had yet seen, a spreading whitewashed establishment, surrounded by manicured gardens. The hard part, as it had been in Nassau, was the walk to the front door and confrontation with the staff. In this case, a butler wearing such a grand coat that Scarlet could have mistaken him for the King himself.

She raised her chin and glared at him. "We've come to see Governor Wellford."

"And what might your business be?" Clearly the butler did not think an Irishwoman, no matter how grandly she was dressed, could have any real business with his employer.

"I've been sent by the Governor of Nassau. To bring a gift. A right rich gift, if you catch my meaning." Scarlet gave a significant look up the driveway to the chest weighing down the carriage's back springs.

The butler continued to inspect her as if she was some new form of barnacle, until his eyes landed on the ruby. It was a grand ruby. Scarlet saw the avarice flash across his face. "Are your presents only for the Governor?" he asked.

Half of Scarlet's mouth twisted into a smile. "Pay the man, Burgess."

Burgess produced his purse and counted out sovereigns. "Enough," Scarlet commanded, after the sixth. "That's right robbery, that is."

"I will see if his lordship is at home."

Scarlet stuck her foot in the doorway. "Grand. We'll wait inside."

The butler, drew himself up, unwilling to wound his own dignity by wrestling with a woman. Stiffly, he opened the door, led Scarlet and Burgess into a pink-and-gold room, and called up another servant, who stood staring at them as if they were accused of pinching the silver.

"You'd best be bringin' in that chest!" Scarlet shouted after the butler's retreating form.

"Very good," murmured Burgess. "Smooth as bricks."

"We're in, ain't we?"

Scarlet paced around the room, conscious of the eyes of their guard, as Burgess stood in the corner, staring at his own feet. Many of the objects around them were things so useless that Scarlet couldn't imagine going to the trouble of stealing them. Eventually Burgess pulled aside the drapes and looked out. "They still haven't brought the chest in."

A few minutes later the Governor entered.

It could be no other. He was as much grander than Henry Avery as Avery was grander than Scarlet; corpulent, aristocratic, and with clothes that fit perfectly. His wig rested properly on top of his head. He did not bow, and Scarlet did not, either. They looked into each other's eyes.

It was a challenge, and Scarlet could tell that the man was surprised when she stood up to him. No doubt he was also surprised that she did not curtsey. But a pirate bent her knee to no man. Scarlet kept her knees and her back straight an offered an insincere smile.

"Jones tells me that you carry a letter from a Mr. Avery."

Scarlet held her back straight and handed over the paper. Wellford read it and smiled. "So the 'Governor of Nassau', as it were, has a proposition." He looked at Scarlet, looked closely at the ruby, and smiled again. "I was just out on the veranda. Perhaps you'd join me for tea?" Scarlet nodded and followed, Burgess trailing after, head down, ignored.

She had experience now with spindly chairs, and plopped herself down as if it were her own bunk, kicking the trailing skirts out of her way. She watched as Welford glanced at the letter again. "As I understand, it's a right fair offer."

The Lord, dropped the paper, picked up a delicate china cup, inspected the color of the contents, and added milk. "I'm not quite sure it is." The man's eyes were cold as a dead fish, his face unreadable. "Avery wants me to turn openly against the king. That is treason, and punishable by death."

"You ain't being asked to send a declaration, only to play along." Scarlet couldn't help leaning forward. "The King might not like some of the things you been up to, and if you get found out, you're alone. Make a pact with Henry, and there will be those who stand with you."

Welford sniffed. "Honor among thieves? I doubt it. If his word is all he offers, I'm not interested."

No one had offered Scarlet tea, but she snagged a cup and poured her own. "Honor among thieves. Henry Avery's a good man, and he keeps his word."

"Anyone with power understands that one's word cannot be kept under all circumstances."

That made no sense to Scarlet, so she went back to her main argument. "Henry Avery will stand beside you if he says he will."

The Governor's eyes slipped back to the ruby between her breasts. "I don't make deals for promises. But perhaps Mr. Avery is offering some more... exotic reward?"

Scarlet sat up, suddenly self-conscious, covering the low front of her dress with her gloved hand. She scowled. "I'm no man's thing to trade."

Wellford gave a confused look, quickly covered by a haughty sniff. "This conversation is beginning to bore me. Jones will show you out."

A strange sound brought him up short. He stopped, dead still, listening. Scarlet paused as well. Someone was arguing at the door. It would have sounded quite normal down near the docks, but in this grand house the noise was jarringly out of place.

Welford put down his teacup. His face went white and froze completely. Boot-heels tramped through the house, loud on the marble floor. Scarlet stood to face whatever was coming.

The Lord's cold eyes went colder still. He stood and tucked Avery's letter into his sleeve. "You whore," he murmured, turning to Scarlet. "You had better not be the cause of this."

The Royal Navy burst into the garden, in the form of a gold-laced, blue-coated officer, followed by a squad of cow-faced young Marines. The sight of the uniforms sent a shiver of fear down Scarlet's spine.

Welford's butler dragged at the officer's sleeve, trying to physically hold him back. Burgess melted into the walls. Scarlet braced herself and lifted her chin. Welford stepped forward, one meaty fist clenched. "What is the meaning of this?"

51

The officer looked a right popinjay, blonde and blue with an aristocratic complexion. He clicked his heels and nodded. "Lord Wellford, I presume?"

Wellford went pink around the jowls. "Who are you, boy?"

"Captain Robert Davenport of His Majesty's Royal Navy. I come bearing your replacement form London. Sir, I regret to inform you that you are under arrest. Please do not try to escape. The house is surrounded."

Two marines moved forward and took Wellford by the arms. Scarlet held her breath. All the red uniforms made her want to scream. She kept remembering her childhood, seeing her brothers being dragged away. Her eyes darted for a way out, but the garden around them was walled, and she was trapped inside the dress.

Welford had forgotten her, and she did not know what to do. What would a grand lady do in a situation like this? She stood, shaking at the knees, keeping her head high.

Then Burgess stepped forward. "Captain Davenport, it seems that we are visiting his lordship at a most inconvenient time. May I take Lady Fitzgerald home? Our carriage is right outside."

Scarlet kept the gloved hand at her breast and looked at the officer's feet, trying to appear demure. She could feel the Captain's eyes on her.

His voice was level and not unkind. "I am very sorry to inconvenience you, my lady, but Lord Wellford is under suspicion of crimes against the Crown. I am afraid that everyone in the house must be detained, and the whole house searched. We will try to detain you in comfort. I will need to speak with you and your servant later."

Scarlet couldn't think of anything to say. She kept her eyes down and sniffed. Burgess stepped in and took her arm. "May I take her into the house for a glass of sherry?"

The Captain snapped his fingers and a marine saluted. "Escort the lady into the house."

Scarlet kept her head down and her hand up. Burgess led her into a room at random, turned and shut the door in the marine's face. His face was white and drawn, but he tried to smile. "Shall we be going out the window?"

Scarlet was shaking so badly she had to lean against the wall.

Burgess pulled back the silk drapery and looked out. When he glanced back at Scarlet, he looked shocked for a moment and came back to stand before her. "What's wrong, Captain?"

"They're all around, Burgess. Damned redcoats. All over the house. I can hear them. Blessed Virgin, I don't want to die like this, like a rat in a trap."

Burgess made a helpless gesture with his hands. "They've got no reason to think we've done anything we shouldn't."

Anger began to rise in Scarlet, pushing the fear down. "I'm a known pirate, man! And the *Donnybrook* is a known ship. That bloody captain don't recognize me because he just sailed in from London, but all he needs is to see the right piece of paper, and he'll string me up in the front yard."

Burgess stared at her in confusion. A clock on the wall ticked. Finally he said, "They won't hang us here, Cap'n. They'll have to take us to Port Royal."

Scarlet took a deep breath. Burgess was right. This was a rich man's house, not a peasant's hovel, back in Ireland. It wouldn't be like her brothers, dragged to the nearest tree and hanged without trial or ceremony.

She could breathe.

She could think. "We can't climb out the window."

"Captain, I have a powerful wish to get away from here."

Scarlet's heart was still pounding, but she could feel her hands again. She stripped off the gloves. "No more than myself. Their captain's an English dog, but he's no fool. He'll have the house surrounded. All kinds of rats may try to spring from this trap. He'll want to catch them all."

"And we can't use the carriage. They'll have that." Burgess' eyes widened, "My god! If they ask our driver, he'll tell them we were picked up at the docks."

"They won't be asking questions of a carriage driver until later." Scarlet pressed her hands to her temples. "The man said he'd search the house. What's he searching for?"

"Papers."

"What for?"

"Records of the bribes, how much folk owe, how much gold is kept where."

"They write that down?"

"My account-book back on the *Donnybrook* is enough to hang us all."

Scarlet took a few more minutes to breathe. "You're right, they likely have the carriage. We can't walk out; we'd be obvious as beggars at a fine-dress ball. Wait, how did them damn marines get here?"

"Some kind of cart. Horses, at least."

"Can you ride?"

Burgess swallowed and managed a wan smile. "I'll do fine."

Scarlet bared her teeth. "I can't, either. All right, horses, or a cart. How do we get out of the house?"

"D'you think they'll give us 'til dark?"

"Don't count on it. What about a hostage?" She paced, dragging her fine skirts, then paused. "We could kidnap the Lord himself! He'll know the house, and want to get away, so he'll cooperate. They won't want to kill 'em outright, he's a bleedin' noble."

"Hostages? Oh, no. I'm not the man you want for this." Burgess wiped his glasses on the hem of his neckcloth. "I'm a bookkeeper."

"You're the man I've got. And you're a pirate. Remember that."

⌘

They could hear servants trotting back and forth, or whispering in the hall. After a while, a chambermaid came in to check on "Lady Fitzgerald." Burgess took her hand, expressed his deep concern for their host, and finally persuaded her to tell him where Lord Wellford was being held.

"Them marines are all over the house, digging into every drawer." The maid was young, and looked worried. "They keep finding papers, and takin' 'em into the office, for that there officer to look at 'em. They're overturning everything; it'll take days to clean it up. And the poor Master, he's shut up in 'is bedchamber, under guard, like some kind of criminal."

When she had told all she knew, Burgess opened the door and gently pushed her out into the hall. Scarlet saw the young marine craning his neck to stare into the room. Spotting an opportunity, she pushed Burgess away from the door, fluttered her eyelashes and asked the young marine into the room for a moment.

He came, touching his hat to her. She smiled into his eyes, backed up to a table, picked up a bronze statue, and clubbed him on the head.

He hit the floor like a rag-doll, still clutching his musket.

"We're committed now." Burgess murmured.

"We were committed the minute that bloody captain walked in here. Just act like nothin's wrong."

Scarlet glanced out into the hall, saw no one else, and then led the way up the stairs, holding up her skirts and focusing on the doorway where two marines stood on guard. Close in, she began to sashay and simper. "My, ain't you fellers handsome?"

The shock on the marines' faces was a rare treat, almost as good as when Burgess walked up and hit the first one with the statue. Scarlet kneed the other one in the groin, then elbowed him on the back of the skull.

The door they had been guarding wasn't even locked. She turned the latch and started to walk in, only to notice that Burgess was still standing in the hallway, his face green.

Scarlet grabbed him by the elbow and dragged him into the room. "What the Bejanx you think you're doing?"

"His head. It was all... I think he's..."

"Killed him, did you?" Scarlet clucked in sympathy. "Well, that's your first one. He would have killed you, sure as sunrise. Come on, now."

The maid had said "bedroom," but it was two rooms together. Wellford was pacing the outer room, staring out the window. He turned at the sound of their footsteps. "What the devil are you doing in here?"

"We're saving your arse." Scarlet smiled. "I figure we've got no more than five minutes until the dead men outside this room get noticed. You're our hostage. We need to get out of this room and around back to the stables. Then it's down to the docks and a fine cruise in the sweetest sloop you'll ever see."

She looked Welford dead in the eyes. "I need them to think that I threaten your life, for until you're tried for treason, your life is worth a lot. After, it'll be worth nothing. I don't suppose you keep pistols in this room?"

"Now see here! This is nothing but a misunderstanding. I'm a wealthy man. The captain will see reason."

Scarlet scowled. "The hell he will. Folk all the way to New Providence know what you've been up to. Avery reckons it's treason, already. That's why he figured the two of you might be friends."

"You little..."

Wellford drew back his hand to slap her, but Scarlet caught his sleeve and glared into his eyes. "Your lordship has committed treason, and is liable to hang."

For a moment Scarlet thought the man would tear loose and strike her. Then sweat broke out on his forehead and jowls, and he glanced desperately around the room. "My god... My god..."

Burgess stepped forward. "Sir. If I may..."

Wellford looked up.

"As we say back in Ireland, my lord, you might as well be hanged for a sheep as hanged for a lamb. That money is still on the back of the carriage. And it's still yours if you throw in with Avery."

"It is?"

Scarlet had no idea if it was or not, but she nodded emphatically. "I've heard what folk make in government. That chest must hold at least four years of your legal salary. Give us a try, love."

Wellford looked at the ruby around at her throat. "Yes. It would be a thing to build on. I could... I could... All right. All right, I'll come."

Scarlet could swear she heard footsteps in the hall, but it might just be her nerves. "Do you keep any pistols hereabouts?"

Welford looked at her as if she was asking for a wedding-cake, and she resisted the urge to punch him. "Well then, we'll use this." Scarlet twisted her arms around to her back and dug her fingers between the lacings in the back of her dress. After a few seconds she withdrew an eight-inch iron spike, sharp as a needle at one end, blunted like the head of a nail on the other. She held it up before the lord's face.

"Ever see a marlin spike before?" she asked. "They're right useful for rigging a ship. The best way to kill a man with one is to drive the sharp end right through his temple. I'll just hold it up to your neck, if we meet with trouble. Now, which way out of the house?"

Wellford looked into Scarlet's eyes, then at the flashing ruby necklace. "Very well. If you think you can actually get me out."

"Tell us the way out of here, to horses or into a carriage. We'll do the rest."

Once again, they walked boldly out into the hall. Wellford blanched at the sight of the dead men. Scarlet felt her pulse jump, but held fast.

"Servant's door. I've no idea what's beyond it." Wellford indicated a section of paneling, almost invisible against the rest of the wall. Scarlet couldn't work the latch from the outside, but slipped the tip of the marlin spike into the crack and lifted the bolt.

The door led to a dark, narrow staircase. Scarlet pushed Wellford ahead of her and struggled after him, dragging the dress. Halfway down she caught her toe on the hem and fell into Wellford, who cursed and stumbled down the stairs. They tumbled noisily into a sitting room full of people.

Not redcoats or nobles. Scarlet raked her eyes over the startled folk, and recognized a maid's cap. A coachman's coat was draped over the back of a chair. She looked at faces until she saw the tanned one, and recognized the coachman who had driven their rented carriage.

She stamped across the room and jerked him out of his chair, showing him the marlin spike, right next to his eye. "Are the horses still hitched up?"

He nodded, his eyes huge and frightened.

"Now listen up. This is what you will do. You will walk out to where that coach is, get on, and turn it around in the coach yard, like you're taking it back to the livery. If anyone asks you, you tell 'em the coach was only rented a couple of hours, and you got to go back. If they press, you tell 'em it's already cleared with... with..." She turned back to Burgess. "What's that blackguard's name?"

"Davenport."

"Right. Captain Davenport. You got that? Then bring the coach to the servant's door, and we'll get in. And if you don't do it, if you have some grand idea of being a hero, then know this." She glared at him. "There's a ship full of desperate men in the harbor, and if I am taken, they will hunt you down, and they will kill you slow. You and your wife and your mother and any little brats you may have rolling around on your floor at home. Do you believe me?"

Another jerky nod. The man's breath already smelled of bile. Scarlet threw him toward the door.

"And take your bloody coat with you." Burgess threw the coat. The coachman took it and stumbled out and up a short flight of steps to ground level.

The door didn't latch when it closed. It swung open, letting in sunlight and the sound of footsteps on gravel. Scarlet felt her heart beating, too fast, too hard. She glared around the room. The servants dropped their eyes and stared at whatever was in front of them.

Finally Scarlet couldn't stand it. She grabbed Wellford by the elbow, and tried to steer him toward the door. He balked until she hissed, "Play along, damn you."

He glared, jowls red as a rooster's crest. Scarlet brought the marlin spike up. That caught his eye, but he was still angry, still fighting her, in his mind if not in his body. She grabbed his wrist and held it, showing the strength she had built up from a lifetime of hard work. A little of the fight went out of him. Together they moved toward the door.

The coachman had climbed up to his seat, but a marine stood in front of the carriage, trying to catch the horses' bridles. The animals, perhaps sensing their driver's fear, reared and neighed.

Wellford tensed and tried to draw away. Scarlet muttered, "Looks like we got to go to them. I'll hold your arm behind you and the spike at your neck. It's your job to play along. With me?"

"You should have taken one of the muskets. You could pick him off from here."

"Take a musket, cartridge case, shot bag and powder horn off a dead man in a corridor? We'd be hanged sure. Come on, move." Scarlet glanced at Burgess once, then headed out into the carriage yard.

Wellford was taller and vastly wider. Scarlet gripped him by the coat sleeve, for her hand wouldn't go all the way around his wrist, and rested the hand with the marlin spike on his shoulder. She could hear Burgess behind.

When they were ten feet into the yard, Captain Davenport came around an ornamental hedge. "What's this?" His stark blue eyes took in the scene at once: Wellford with the spike at his throat, Scarlet right behind, her hair tumbled around her shoulders, dress torn, eyes wild.

"Help!" shouted Wellford, jerking away hard. "The bloody bitch is trying to kidnap me!"

"Unhand his lordship!" Davenport bellowed, drawing his sword.

Wellford pulled like a wild horse. Scarlet could barely hold him. A dragging edge of skirt came under her feet. She stumbled, stepped on it and felt it rip away. "Stay away from us," she ordered Davenport. "If you come closer, I'll kill him."

"She's a pirate! They're trying to frame me. Help!" Wellford jerked and tried to twist away. Scarlet clung to him desperately. Then Burgess grabbed the other arm and together they had him.

Scarlet glared into the captain's eyes. "We'll be getting into that carriage, and you won't stop us. Not if you don't want a dead lord on your hands."

Davenport stepped closer. "If I let you go, you'll kill him in the carriage." The marine stopped upsetting the horses, and aimed his musket.

Scarlet kept her eyes away from the Marine in the red uniform. She held Davenport's eyes. "My word, if you let us go, he'll live."

"You, madam, are a pirate."

"And you, milord, are a milk-faced prig with a mainspar up your arse."

Scarlet and Burgess inched Wellford closer to the carriage. "Pockets, Mister Burgess," Scarlet whispered. "A pistol would come quite handy right now."

"Oh, my goodness. I forgot." Scarlet heard Burgess rummaging in his own pocket, and then the click of a pistol being cocked.

"Been nice to have it earlier."

"I'm sorry, Captain," he squeaked.

Scarlet could see Burgess' arm waving as he tried to aim the pistol at everyone at once. She smiled at Davenport. "Now we have a problem. Mister Burgess here knows not a bloody thing about firearms. The one in his hand could go off at any time, and kill anybody here. I've nothing to lose. How about yourself?"

"I am a King's officer, and will do my duty."

"You've arrested your man. I'm sure he's left a powerful lot of ill-gotten gold for the Crown to reclaim. Ain't that enough?"

"My duty, woman, is to bring him to trial."

Davenport walked toward them crabwise, careful of his feet like a good fighter, trying to get between the pirates and the carriage. The marine stood his ground like an idiot, unable to shoot past Wellford's corpulent form.

Scarlet pressed the spike against Wellford's neck until a drop of blood stained his perfect linen shirt. "Burgess," she said, "kindly shoot the lobster. We will pick up his musket as we move past."

The pistol went off with a loud "pang!" and a great puff of white smoke. The marine's hat blew off, and he threw his weapon into the air in panic.

The horses reared and surged forward, sending the marine flying, despite the coachman's frantic efforts with the reins. He gained control of the team just as the lead animals came between the pirates and Davenport's sword.

"Into the carriage, quick!" called Scarlet, as she snatched up the fallen musket.

Davenport grasped the lead horse's reigns with a firm hand and gave a low-voiced command. "Be still!" The horse went stiff as a statue, shaking in every limb.

Scarlet and Davenport met in front of the team, he with sword drawn, she with the musket leveled at his guts. She pulled the trigger, but something had broken when the gun fell, and she got no more than a click. He braced himself to slash at her.

She parried with the musket, and they glared into each other's eyes, shoving strength against strength for one moment. He was a tall man and strong, but Scarlet had spent a lifetime hauling ropes and sail, and for that moment her rage and fear held him.

Then the westering sun caught the ruby at Scarlet's throat. When it flashed, the red light struck Davenport in the eye and he flinched. It was enough. Scarlet gave back, and he fell forward, stumbling. The horses knocked both of them down, but Scarlet was on the side of the open carriage door. She caught it and scrambled in.

The carriage barely made the turn onto the driveway, and ploughed through a half-dozen marines on the way to the front gate. The horses were outside of anyone's control, and when they reached the road they turned downhill, toward the harbor and their own stable.

The carriage made it to the seedier part of town before it

overturned. Scarlet crawled from the wreck and laughed, laughed until her sides hurt and her head spun.

"What's so bloody funny?" Wellford had probably never been handled so roughly in his life. He managed to look frightened, rumpled and angry, all at the same time. Mostly angry. Seeing his purple jowls, Scarlet laughed even harder.

"Well?"

"We're all alive for the next hour or so, and at the moment, I can ask no more. C'mon, Welly, smile. The Royal Navy ain't got you now."

Lord Wellford twitched his clothing back into some semblance of order, grumbling.

When Scarlet had helped Burgess out the carriage door, she went round to have a look at the coachman. The fellow was just stirring, having taken a blow to the head, and Scarlet offered him her hand.

When he saw her he fell back in fear, but she took the hand all the same. "Up with you. Feeling well?" The pupils in his frightened eyes were both the same size. He was probably unharmed. Scarlet pulled him to his feet. "Mister Burgess, have you got any money about you?"

"Sorry ma'am."

Scarlet thought for a moment, then stripped off her pearl earrings and pressed then into the coachman's hand. "Here. For your trouble."

She turned to the others. "Let's be off, then."

They pushed their way past the crowd that was gathering around the wrecked coach and headed off down a side street. Burgess turned to stare at the chest of gold. "Do we leave it here?"

Welford started to speak, but Scarlet cut him off. "That money loose in a crowd will keep the bloody Captain off our heels better than anything. Let it lie."

Welford glared. She glared back and went on. "Do you want to stay here with it? Them Marines will be here in a minute."

All color drained out of the man and he backed away.

Scarlet pointed ahead. "You can see the masts from here. We need to split up and get to the *Donnybrook*. Burgess, go on ahead. You look less like a pirate than anyone I know. His lordship here is going to play at being very drunk, and I am going to play his doxie. No one should notice us."

Scarlet knew she looked a sight, for her hair was straggling in elf-locks and the grand dress had aged twenty years in the last hour. Ripped bits of it fluttered all around. She reached up and pulled Wellford's head down to her throat and began to stagger toward the docks and safety.

Halfway to their goal, the man pulled her into a stinking alleyway and began to kiss her in earnest. Scarlet let him for a few moments as she eyed the street for someone caught wise, but when his hands began ripping fabric, she pushed him away.

"What do you think you're about?"

His face was slack and his eyes burned. "Damn you! You cost me everything. It's all your fault those bloody marines showed up. Now you'll give me something back."

She shoved him, hard. "It's you as brought 'em in. Get off me. We need to get out of here, before the Royal Navy shows up."

In answer, he put his face down and began to lick her, just where the ruby rested.

She pushed him away, and when he tried to grab her, slapped him hard. He stood staring, jaw slack, eyes focused on the necklace around her throat.

The ruby seemed to have some grasp on Welford. Scarlet didn't know why, but there was not time to wonder. She jerked the necklace off, breaking the clasp, and dropped the necklace down between her breasts.

At once, Wellford seemed to come to himself. "What are we doing here? Why aren't we going to the ship?"

"You're the one footling around. Cut the shite and move."

They were four blocks from the bustling pier. Scarlet grabbed him by the sleeve and walked.

No one stopped them. Scarlet felt the fear rising and rising with every step, down to the dockyard, out onto the pier. Coming closer and closer to the ship, terrified that a man in a red coat would step into her path. Reaching the *Donnybrook*'s deck felt like paradise.

The crew gathered round at once, but first Scarlet had questions. "Has Burgess got here yet? Where's the Navy?"

Burgess shouldered his way through the crowd. "I'm all right. I told them to be ready to cast off."

Pryce cut him off. "There's a Navy frigate in this port, Cap'n, and her captain came tearing in on horseback twenty minutes back. They've already cast off, and they're taking her out to the mouth of the harbor. They mean keep us bottled up in here."

Scarlet peered out, but night was falling fast, and fog obscured everything. She could barely make out a ship's lights, deep in the mist. "We can slip past them."

A bell rang, deep but brisk. "But Cap'n," Pryce said, "We darn't run with no lights at all. Half the folk in this harbor are smugglers, or worse. Everyone's trying to run off. If we collide with someone, we could break open and be in worse shape than we are."

Lord Wellford puffed himself up. "You promised me, you trollop, that you would get me safe out of this port."

Scarlet scanned the deck. "Mister Yeboah, take this man below, gag him and throw him in the brig." The *Donny's* huge crewmember bore down on the lord with a smile, and Wellford quailed.

As Wellford was hauled below, Scarlet looked at all the anxious faces. "I need to get out of this damned dress and think.

Don't cast off until I say. Mister Pryce, please help me with this wretched thing."

In her cabin, Scarlet leaned against the bulkhead and sighed, while Pryce bent over the lacings behind her. "Pryce, this Navy ship... How big? Could we take her?"

"No, ma'am, we could not. It's a frigate, with thirty guns at least. We'd need a very different boat to take her on."

"Mary, Mother of God, but I'm tired." The dress came open in the back, and Scarlet caught the ruby in her hand. If the frigate kept the harbor bottled up, then soldiers could search every ship in the morning. It wouldn't take long to single them out. In fact, simply asking the harbormaster, "Are there any vessels with red-headed female captains?" would get Davenport what he wanted. No, they must somehow get past Davenport in the dark.

Looking deep into the glowing gem, Scarlet felt her determination rising. She would not die. She would not let her crew be hanged. She would not let Henry Avery down. There had to be a way.

"We would need a different boat."

With shaking hands, Scarlet drew on breeches and a shirt. Suddenly she had an idea.

Back on deck, she gave out orders, quietly but firmly. "I want two of them spare spars lashed together and set crosswise, about eight feet above our stern. I want a lantern hung eight feet above the very tip of our bowsprit. Mr. Burgess, do you remember the ship's bell we took off that Bristol packet? The pretty one, with the mermaids on it? Dig that out of the hold."

"How?"

"Why?"

"I don't rightly know where it is, Captain."

"You're sailors. You know rigging and line. Figure it out. Because I said so. And Burgess, we need a deeper-toned bell, and we need it now."

As the crew worked, she outlined her plan. They would hang lanterns at the very perimeters of the *Donnybrook*, making her seem both taller and longer in the mist. The deeper ship's bell would add to the illusion. As they bore up to the Navy ship, they would hail her and claim to be an East India trader, a ship that even the Navy would hesitate to fire upon.

"If we can get abreast of her, we'll turn and run. We can turn twice as tight as any square-rigger ever made, and sail eight points closer to the wind. We'll tack all the way back to Nassau."

The crew set to work, and Scarlet stared into the fog, remembering the layout of the docks and harbor, and trying to imagine where a Navy man would lay to bottle the place up. "Lower the longboat, too. We'll take a tow. Just run a line to the rail, and keep the boat on our starboard side."

The longboat started them moving. Three lanterns hung in a row high above the *Donnybrook*'s stern, looking like lights along the back rail, and a single one floated ghostly above the bowsprit. With this disguise she could pass for a ship twice her size. Burgess came huffing up the ladder with the bell, and as soon as it was on the deck, Scarlet set William to tapping it, two fast ones, and then a wait, then two quick again.

The longboat helped them along, but the evening breeze had sprung up, ready to take them out to sea. At first the sounds of other ships were all around, but gradually, slowly, the noise faded as they left the dock and slipped out into the harbor.

"Bring the boat up," Scarlet ordered softly.

Everyone on deck kept falling silent, but Scarlet motioned them to keep talking and make the usual ship's noises. Then, as the *Donnybrook* came up on the stern lights of the Navy ship, a voice called out. "Ahoy! Unknown ship! Identify yourself!"

Scarlet had been planning for this. Her Gunnery Master, Edric Bracegirdle, had a deeply English tone and a barrel chest. He stood on the deck beside her, and she whispered what she wanted him to repeat. Nothing would sound so respectable as Bracegirdle's authoritative, middle-class bellow. "Ahoy! We are the East India trader *Boulder* bound for the Carolinas. Please identify yourself."

The answer came with hardly any delay. "We are the *HMS Nightingale*, in His Majesty's service. The mouth of this port is closed until further notice. Turn back."

Scarlet kept realizing that she was holding her breath. Her chest felt heavy, and it was hard to breathe. She whispered again to Bracegirdle, who bellowed like a real officer. "*HMS Nightingale*, we are unable to comply."

"*Boulder*, turn back, or you will be fired upon."

The frigate loomed before them, close enough that its outline could be seen through the fog. Scarlet whispered and Bracegirdle shouted. "*Nightingale*, we are required to make rendezvous with our convoy tomorrow noon."

"Turn back. This is your last warning."

An explosion. Red fire shot out from the *Nightingale*, and Scarlet heard the whistle of a cannon ball going across their bow.

This was it. This was the place where Scarlet's plan either got them into open water or killed everyone on board. She only hoped that Davenport had drilled his men well in their gun-practice.

Scarlet could feel the rush of water under the bow change, as they came up on the mouth of the harbor. They were so close she could hear counting on the *Nightingale*. "Everyone, <u>down!</u>" she roared at the top of her voice, just as the broadside boomed out, spitting fire and blowing smoke.

The sound of the guns made Scarlet's head ring. She heard someone scream, and the sound of tearing canvas.

But when she looked up, The *Donnybrook* and her sails were almost entirely intact. The English gunners had been as accurate as their reputation. If the *Donny* had been galley rigged, or frigate-rigged, or as big as they had disguised her to be, there would have been broken masts all over the deck. But the *Donny* was a sloop, with her mainmast in different location entirely. She had lost a little canvas, but that could be fixed with a needle and thread.

A cheer went up, and just then the wind surged, and the fog began to tear into scraps. Scarlet shouted "Hard a-port!" and the *Donnybrook* skimmed, smooth as silk, right before the *Nightingale*'s bow, close enough that Scarlet could make a rude gesture at Davenport as they slid past and shout "Mary's grace upon ye!"

After that they let out the flying jib, and sailed into the wind's teeth, leaving the *Nightingale* far behind.

⌘

"I'm right sorry, sir, that we did not succeed in getting the alliance. But we brung you a present."

Scarlet stood on the carpet in front or Henry Avery's fine desk, and as she spoke, she pulled the hood off her captive to reveal Wellford's spluttering face.

Wellford glared, then drew himself up to his full height and shouted, "I demand that this woman be punished…"

"He's been like this." Scarlet explained. "Has no grasp of the fact that he's wanted by the Crown, and is not much use to us. But the Crown may pay to get him back. They might as well pay you. I turn him over, in hopes he may be of value."

Avery looked at Wellford, then at Scarlet. "Jacobson," he called into the next room. "Get in here and take our guest upstairs."

A man in livery came in and escorted Wellford from the room. Avery turned back to Scarlet, stared at her, and finally said, "I thank you for your efforts, Captain MacGrath. Now, do you care to return my ruby necklace?"

Scarlet bowed. "I had hoped that it was a present, sir, but brought it with me all the same. I'm afraid the clasp is broken."

She poured the stream of gems and gold into his hands, then paused to look at it wistfully. "Ther's something to it, ain't there? It does something. I felt it, but I could never figure it out."

"I believe it is." Avery slipped the necklace into a waiting velvet bag. "I think it causes a person to *want* more sharply, to desire what he already desired, but to the point of madness. I had hoped that it would inspire our friend here in his greed."

Scarlet glanced after Wellford. "He's greedy for too many things, is the problem. For money and power and sex. He wouldn't have been a good ally."

"Maybe not. But we're still an island alone. And you say there's a new frigate in the Carrib?"

"The *Nightengale*. And she's a beautiful as her name, from what I could see."

"Her commander?"

"Name's Davenport. An intelligent man. Could be a lot of trouble for us."

Avery frowned, then put the velvet bag in his desk. "We'll see. Now, come and have supper with me. You must tell me about this frigate. Welford will wait upstairs – probably for a good long time."

"Aye, sir."

⌘

Robert Davenport sat in his cabin, staring out into the night. He had not eaten dinner, and Hughes, his steward, had clucked protectively as he carried away the uneaten food. Robert chose not to notice.

He had a report to write, and it would not be pleasant. He had been sent on a simple mission, to arrest a man, and to gather evidence for a trial, and instead he had been out-maneuvered, out-fought and out-run by a bog-trotting Irish female, apparently the captain of a pirate ship.

He had hoped that being assigned to the many islands of the Caribbean would give him some chance of a social life, some opportunity to meet an Englishwoman of decent family, and to have enough time on land to court her and obtain a wife. Indeed, he had lobbied for the opportunity.

Instead, he had been outsmarted. Nay, defeated. He could scarcely hold his head up. He might even be recalled in disgrace. This did not bode well for social introductions. He might be alone forever.

And worse, he kept thinking of the girl herself. Little more than a cheeky chit, really. But her eyes had been so very, very green.

He remembered those green eyes. And the flashing ruby she had worn around her throat.

The Captives

The sky above was blue, but the horizon was black, and ugly bands of steel-gray clouds lay between them. The *Donnybrook* heeled so far to starboard as she ran that water washed up over the rail.

Scarlet stood on the deck, hauling with her crew, trying to shift the cannons to port and better balance the ship against the force of the wind. She could hear the decks rumble as Mister Burgess shifted cargo below-decks for the same purpose. Her hands were full, but her eyes kept being drawn upward, to the huge white sails stretched to their maximum, and the groaning wood of the mast.

Her instinct was to put on every inch of canvas and fly before the wind like a gull, evading the monstrous storm behind them. But she had an old gaff and a new mainsail, and she needed to gauge whether the sail would split, or the gaff be carried away by the strain.

The sweating sailors hauled the last of the cannons to the port rails and stayed themselves, adding their weight. The angle of the deck changed several degrees and Scarlet nodded to herself. Then she looked at the sky to larboard, went to Flynn and shouted at the top of her lungs, "Reef sail!"

He shouted back a question, but she couldn't hear him over the increasing sound of the wind. Guessing, she held up two fingers. He nodded and set the men to work. Two reefs in the mainsail.

Scarlet clawed her way up to the quarterdeck and leaned in to help Pryce hold the wheel. "Still on course?" she bellowed.

Pryce nodded, taking one of her hands off the wheel to point. At least they had a goal, a series of tiny islands southeast of Hispaniola, some little more than rocks, others large enough to shelter a ship. This ship if they were lucky.

When the first band of gray cloud came overhead the rain came with it, slashing like cat's claws and cold as an Englishman's heart. Visibility dropped and Scarlet cupped a hand to the side of Pryce's head to shout, "Take in mainsail, reef fore headsail!" Pryce nodded and staggered forward to convey the order, her slender form bowed against the wind, her long hair uncoiled and twisting.

Now they would simply have to endure it. In this rain, visibility was near to nothing. Scarlet knew this part of the Caribbean well, and she had planned to come up on the lee side of the islands; to shelter behind them. But if her calculations were wrong, there might be land to the lee of them, instead of good empty sea. It would do them no good to run aground. The *Donnybrook* only drew eight feet, but they wouldn't have even that under her keel if they ran into the side of an island.

Scarlet tried to keep them on course by the compass reading and the sight of blue sky receding before them. At times she believed she could glimpse the islands, and at others she thought there were only the waves.

Then the first band of weather passed them by, and Scarlet could see land, jutting out of the ocean before them, big enough to shelter a dozen ships. Scarlet called to Flynn to haul sail, and spun the wheel. Every timber of the *Donny* creaked, and after a breathless hour they were in the lee of land.

It was the spot she had been aiming for, a wide volcanic island with a sheltered cove to the southeast. Scarlet found the cove's mouth and put the *Donnybrook* in it, in shallow water, then called for the anchors to drop.

"Reef all sails!" she called. "Let's batten these cannons down. Square her away, and we'll ride it out in our own bunks." The second squall hit just as the cannon were lashed down again. Scarlet kept the men out in the slashing rain until both anchors were properly set down onto a coral bottom, the *Donnybrook* situated between them, and everything battened down properly. Only then did they head below.

Scarlet was as wet as if she'd been swimming. As soon as she closed the cabin door behind her she wrung out her clothes and threw them into a bucket. The cabin was a mess. Her big desk, captain's bunk and her sea chest were the only things that hadn't been loose or broken loose, and furniture and objects had piled along the starboard bulkhead like driftwood.

Scarlet found slop trousers and a shirt that were only humid, not awash, and slipped into them. The deck under her feet, now level, had developed a regular pitch-and-yaw movement as the ship rode the waves under control of the anchor cables. Perhaps when she had cleared away she would sling her hammock and forgo the bunk for the night.

Something tapped on her door, so soft that the sound was almost lost in the *Donny*'s creaking.

"Come."

Mister Yeboah opened the door, looking sheepish and very wet. "Don't mean to disturb you, Captain."

"Out with it, man. You're dripping on my deck."

"You have a light here, ma'am? It's terrible dark below."

Scarlet nodded to the lantern swinging above them. "I do. Ain't they got candles?"

"A few, ma'am. It's dark, though." Yeboah shifted his vast bulk nervously. "De storm scares me, ma'am."

Scarlet sighed. Her newest crewmember was the largest human that she had ever seen, tall, wide in the shoulders, crowded with muscle, and why he should be afraid of anything was beyond her. "Stay if you like. Don't you have any dry clothes?"

"No ma'am."

Scarlet pulled a blanket off the bunk. "Here, wrap up in this." She'd have to see about more clothes for the man. Most of her crew had stacks of clothing, finery and work things, but Yeboah was too large to fit into stolen garments. He was too large to fit most places. "If you stay here, you'll have to bunk down on the deck."

The huge man nodded and curled up along the aft bulkhead.

"Excuse me, Cap'n?" The Shantyman knocked and entered. He was, if possible, wetter than Yeboah.

"Do you think you could manage to drag a bit more of the sea in here? This cabin was half-dry a minute ago."

The Shantyman gave a courtier's bow. "My regrets, ma'am, but as I was up on deck just now, trying to catch some wind in me cord, I seen another ship come into this cove. Thought you should know."

"What's she look like?"

"About our size, I think a sloop. But it's so black out there you can't see a hand before ye."

"Well, then it's either a fine breakfast or a fight in the morning. Will you be going down below, or stay up here and slop more water about?"

"There's a barrel of brandy open for the crew, so I don't think I'll tarry."

Scarlet spent a damp and wakeful night, dreaming of navy ships and treasure sloops, and jumping awake every time the wind changed.

Dawn found her back on the deck. Though the wind was still strong, the rain had fallen off to ragged sheets, and as the sun rose Scarlet was able to distinguish the features of the other ship. Sloop-rigged with square topsail, and fancywork around her railing. She risked a shout. "Ho!" Then again. "Ahoy!"

A man came out on deck and waved. Scarlet stood out where he could see her and whooped. She kicked open the hatch and shouted down below, "Get up here, you lubbers! It's Black Sam in the *Bathsheba!*"

They drew the two ships together and lashed them as tight as they would go, and while the sailors traded boasts and hung sails out to dry, Scarlet climbed over and threw herself in Sam Bellamy's arms.

"Sam, it's good to see you!"

His smile was white against his dark skin, darker where the beard showed under his clean-shaven cheeks, and his blue eyes danced. His pigtail had come undone, and black hair brushed the shoulders of his bottle-green coat. "And you, beautiful Scarlet! Don't you look fine?"

"Not as good as you, Sam." Scarlet ran a hand through her hair. "Rough night last night."

"Aye. Thought we were for it."

"Everyone all right? Where are Cap'n Horner and Eddie?"

"Ah, nothing's wrong. They took the *Carthage* up to New Orleans. Some hoo-doo woman that Eddie wanted to talk to. But you're just the person I wanted to see. Before that blow come in, I was chasing a pretty Dutch schooner, three masts, but riding low in the water. I figure she's got a belly full of goods, and was just waiting to turn 'em over to me. Would you like to come along?"

"You're the luckiest man in all the Caribbean. Of course I want to be in on the haul. I just hope she didn't fly away from us, or break in pieces."

"We'll see, we'll see. You breakfast yet?"

"Our cookfire's out."

"Then come have sausages and tea."

The *Bathsheba's* cabin was larger than Scarlet's own, but offered less headroom. Sam had to duck under the beams. He found Scarlet a chair in front of the teapot, then disappeared for a moment and returned with two sizzling plates.

"The *Donnybrook* looks as lovely as her captain. New paint?"

Scarlet nodded and swallowed. "Got it in Nassau. Avery traded me for an errand."

"I told him you'd be perfect for that. Do we have Tortuga on our side?"

"As it was politics, I should have known you was involved. I took Avery's letter, but Governor Wellford had no chance to come over. The English had found him out, probably months ago. They'd recalled him, and sent a replacement from London. I got there ten minutes before a navy captain and the royal marines showed up. Did get Wellford out. Avery's ransoming him back to the Crown now. They'll probably hang him."

"Damn."

"Good sausages, these."

Sam stabbed a sausage. "It'll take months to feel out the new governor. And Port Royal's secure in Crown hands. The whole pirate fleet couldn't take that island."

Scarlet barked a laugh. "Since when are we a fleet?"

"We would be if we ever stood together. How many guns do we have? And how many fight for the Crown?"

"About thirty more than used to. New governor come over on a sixth-rate. The *Nightingale* she's called. Brand new. Not as big as the *Falcon* but beautiful lines. Commander's named... wait, let me think… Davenport. Stiff, he is. I tricked my way around him in the fog."

Sam sipped his tea, looking thoughtful. "They say Ned Doyle caught himself a slaver, a right fine ship."

"He did. And tried to make war on the Donnelly boys with it. But the ship was haunted, and she's at the bottom of Donnelly's cove now. Ned's lucky Conner Donnelly has a wide streak of mercy. Let the *Cardiff Rose* come and pick him up after the slaver was sunk."

"I've a mind to pick me up a slaver, one of these days."

Scarlet chewed her sausage and thought. "It was a grand ship, but full of ghosts. I wouldn't sail in a slave ship."

"Well, if I was to catch one, I'd find a way to lay all her ghosts. Pay back some of the folks who deal in slaves."

Scarlet smiled.

"May I ask you a thing? Everyone says you bewitched Ned, something about spirits."

It didn't take much – it was the men's own guilt that done them in."

Sam looked serious. "Can you do that, and be a good Catholic besides? Everyone says you take it serious."

Scarlet showed him the St. Bridged's medal on its string, then kissed it and put it back in her bosom. "St. Bridged was a pagan goddess long before she was a saint. I'm trusting to her good will."

"I don't understand any of it, but I imagine we'll all meet in hell." Sam stood up and wiped his mouth on his sleeve. "Ready to go hunting, dear?"

⌘

The two ships set out in the direction the schooner's last heading, and sailed parallel, just within sight of each other. Every eye was trained on the horizon. The black flag snapped smartly in the stiff breeze.

This area held dozens of islands. Scarlet took in sail, letting the *Bathsheba* get ahead. Sam was lucky, everybody knew that, but she didn't feel her own luck was with her today. No reason to bump along the side of something solid. They might cruise a couple of days, looking for their prey.

As they came up on a rocky isle, Sam signaled to the *Donnybrook* that they should come closer together. Scarlet believed that she knew his mind. As they had sheltered from the storm behind a spot of land, so the schooner might have sheltered here. With a little grace, the ship might still be nearby.

Sam came near, to pass the isle on the windward side, and Scarlet went to the lee, letting sails out as they lost wind to the island. The isle was mountainous, a great pile of rock towering high, with only a few scattered palms and wild grasses showing green. The southwest sea was dark with the island's shadow.

A ship hid in that shadow. A woman along the *Donny*'s rail let out a whoop at first, and the rest took it up. But then Scarlet spun the wheel and began to shout orders, for the vessel hiding in the shade was no Dutch schooner, but something more familiar and more deadly. The Navy frigate *Falcon* had no other purpose than to hunt pirates.

In that instant the *Donnybrook* turned from predator to prey. The *Falcon* out rated her by a hundred and fifty tons, stood ten feet higher out of the water, and carried twenty more cannon and over a hundred more crew. She could crush the *Donnybrook* like an egg.

Scarlet bellowed, "Run up the gaff topsail! Raise fore staysail!" Crew scrambled to the rigging, and the Shantyman began a chant, to keep them all in time together as they hauled.

The frigate must have been just casting off. She was underway before Scarlet would have believed possible, showing a vast cloud of white canvas. In a straight run, the larger ship would be faster.

Scarlet wanted to turn and run into the wind. It was her ship's strongest point, a feat no square-rigger could match. But the *Falcon* was upwind, and the *Donnybrook* needed more sailing room to get clear and come about. They didn't have it, the *Falcon* was too close. Another island loomed on the horizon.

"Where's Sam?" Scarlet called up to Sunny Jim in the lookout's perch.

A pause, then, "He's coming up behind the *Falcon*! I think he means to fire on her. He's signaling, too, but I can't read it, the navy's in the way."

Good old Sam. If he attacked fearlessly enough, and signaled hard enough, he might convince the navy captain that they had a fleet of pirate ships. Everyone knew the *Bathsheba* seldom traveled without the *Carthage*. Alone, the *Donnybrook* was helpless before the bigger ship. With the *Bathsheba* she had a prayer. If the navy captain believed more pirates were on their way, he might consider himself outnumbered. He might break off and go home.

"Load the guns!" Scarlet called. The *Falcon* was bearing down on them. There were uncharted reefs all over the place. They would have to trust to the *Donny's* shallow draft coming around the islet.

The island loomed suddenly large. Scarlet could see the white of the sea bottom, so close to the surface it seemed she could reach down and touch it. The *Falcon* was nearly within gun range. "Ready the boom!" She would swing as close to land as she dared. If they didn't ground in the shallows, she could swing to port as soon as they were past the island, and run off due north. The *Falcon* would have to bear farther south to stay in deep water.

Smoke blossomed along the *Falcon's* side, her guns boomed, and cannonballs whistled overhead, tearing up the mainsail but doing little other damage. First broadside. Scarlet gritted her teeth and held her course.

Another roar of cannon hit Scarlet's ears, and bits of the *Donnybrook* exploded in all directions. Scarlet clutched the wheel to hold herself upright as the ship jerked beneath her. She saw blood on the deck, sailors knocked off their feet, rubble suddenly everywhere on what had been an orderly deck. But worst of all, the ship's wheel in her hands went suddenly dead. Something was wrong with the rudder. Her precious *Donnybrook* was disabled.

With no rudder, the wind controlled them, and the *Donnybrook* started to veer off to the south. Scarlet dropped the useless wheel and ran forward. "Get your bloody heads down. Pryce, climb up here and take the wheel. The rudder's shot off. McNamara! Get your bloody tools! I need you down there to check it out. Flynn, get this man below. Mister Yeboah, swing that boom, we've got to get her head up."

Most of the ship seemed intact. Behind them the *Falcon* gave an enormous lurch. Her crew staggered and went down, and the mainmast shuddered. Scarlet could see the officers shouting orders. The larger ship must have run aground.

This bought the pirates precious time, but there was no telling how badly the *Falcon* was hurt. Her crew might float her again. Even the next wave might lift her off. If Scarlet didn't get her rudder working soon, the *Donnybrook* would drift out into the main channel and be easy prey.

They might as well deliver a warning. "Fire starboard guns!"

Bracegirdle got the gun crews to their stations, and the cannons went off, one after the other. Scarlet thought she saw two shots hit home, but at this range they had little real chance of damaging the larger ship.

Then the *Bathsheba* cut in from the north, right across the navy ship's unprotected stern. Scarlet heard the boom of cannons and the higher-pitched clack of muskets and small arms. A great cloud of white smoke rose, and then the *Bathsheba* was clear, coming around for another run. A cheer went up along the *Donnybrook*'s deck. Up close, Sam's cannon had done good work.

"Sail! Sail ho!" Scarlet's lookout was shouting, pointing off northeast. Some new ship was coming into the fight. Scarlet saw square-rigged sails, and thought it might be a brig. If it was a navy ship, they were doomed.

"What's the devil's going on down there?" she shouted down to McNamara, who was hanging off the stern, up to his chest in water, working on the *Donnybrook*'s rudder.

"Rudder-chain's shot up. I'm trying to rig it with rope."

Scarlet calculated. Rope on a rudder would stretch and fray, but it might last for an hour. "How long?"

"Ten minutes."

"Make it less. Company's coming." Scarlet moved forward along the deck and called below, "Sanchez, bring up the pistols and cutlasses. And Mister Burgess, find that rusty rudder-chain we took off in Nassau port."

The *Falcon* lurched over the reef or rock it had hit and began a long, slow turn that would bring her back to fire on Scarlet again. Sam made another run across her stern, taking small arms fire and a shot from a small cannon the navy sailors had dragged to their battered railing. The *Bathsheba* had holes in her sails, but she came on gallantly.

Cannon fire from the north. The brig was closer now, and Scarlet recognized the *Cardiff Rose*, with Red Ned Doyle's crimson pennant flying off her mainmast, and sixty pirates, armed to the teeth, lined up screaming along the rails.

The *Falcon* saw her, too. She never completed the turn, but bore away slowly eastward, leaving the pirates behind.

By the time Ned came up, the *Donnybrook* had anchored, and the crew was setting her to rights. The rigged rudder-rope was being cut away, and the old rusty chain handed down to replace it.

"Are you in need of any assistance, darlin'?" Ned called down to Scarlet.

"Doin' fine, thank you very much."

"Well, as soon as you're finished with that cat's cradle, you should come across and have a drink."

"I'll not be drinking with you any time soon, Ned Doyle. Keep away."

The *Bathsheba* eased her way closer. Scarlet watched her come. She had lost some bits of trim, but her mast still stood tall, and the crew seemed in high spirits. Sam came up by the bowsprit and called out, "Both of you, come aboard. We need to talk."

Ned's dark eyes turned to Sam. "You ain't tellin' me what to do, are you, Mister Bellamy?"

"No, I'm inviting. Would you mind coming over? We have an opportunity. And thanks are in order."

"In a minute." Scarlet stood up from where she had been squatting on the deck. She needed to change clothes. Damned if she was going to meet Ned Doyle in less than her best coat. She wanted pistols and her sword as well.

⌘

When she climbed up the *Bathsheba*'s boarding ladder, Sam and Ned were in the middle of a staring contest. Ned was speaking. "…and when I saw the lady last, she shot me."

"I didn't shoot you very bad, Ned. You're still here to complain of it." Scarlet approached the two men with feigned airiness.

Sam broke out in his easy, winning smile. "And don't you want to thank Captain Doyle for his assistance, Scarlet dear?"

"Thank you kindly, Ned, but I had everything under control." Scarlet glanced across at the relative positions of the two ships. "And I'd thank you again if you'd call over and have your ship stop tryin' to get upwind of mine."

Sam glanced back at the other man. "I'm sure the *Rose* is trying to do no such thing? Is she, Ned?"

"I hadn't thought of it." Ned crossed his arms. "Well, what opportunity were you speakin' about?"

"Come down to my cabin. I have some very fine whiskey."

⌘

With the whiskey poured, and the pleasantries over, Sam put his elbows on the table and leaned forward. "You see what we can accomplish when we work together."

"I wasn't workin' with no one," Ned growled. "I was fighting the English Navy."

"You know full well that frigate could've eaten any one of us alive. But together...."

Scarlet broke in. "I ain't together with Ned Doyle."

"Damn it!" Bellamy pounded on the table. "Don't you want anything more than control of one little ship in all the vast ocean? Don't you want to build something?"

Scarlet frowned. "You sound like that fool, Conner Donnelly."

Ned glared. "One ship, and I do what I please. I don't take orders."

"I'm not asking either of you to take orders. I'm asking you to reach an agreement. You reach agreements with your crews, don't you?"

Stubborn silence.

"Let's try this. Ned, Captain MacGrath and I were searching for a schooner I saw riding low in the water, right before that storm hit. Now, the longer we wait, the more chance she has of getting away, but I have a feeling, and my feelings usually run true. D'you both believe I'm a lucky man?"

"No doubt of that."

"None."

"Then let the three of us chase it. We can cover a lot of sea, and it'd do no harm to have help when we make our run for it. She's big."

Scarlet measured Ned with her eyes. "I'll not be on hand when Red Ned Doyle sacks a ship. Cutting folk up, beating them half to death, after they've surrendered and are handing over the goods, it ain't my way. I won't stand back and see it done."

"Ah, darlin' it helps to speed the process."

Scarlet didn't blink.

"What about if we just string 'em up for a little?" Ned pulled his own neck cloth and mimed the face of a hanged man. "It takes 'em twenty minutes to strangle, generally. I wouldn't haul 'em up for more than ten."

Scarlet could see her brothers again, kicking, struggling, fighting for air, all those many minutes. Her hands and face went numb. "Damn you..."

Sam placed his warm hand over her cold one. "Easy, Scarlet." He turned back to Ned. "I'm asking you now, asking nice. For a fat prize, could you forego your usual tactics? For the lady's favor?"

"And what favor is the lady willin' to give me?"

Scarlet set her jaw.

Sam caught her eyes with his blue ones. "Scarlet?"

"Not what he wants." She glared a Ned again. "If you forego your ways, I'll speak nicely to that brothel-owner in Belize, the one that threw you out. She's still offering a hundred pounds for your head. Or other parts."

"That's not much."

"It's two hours of good behavior."

Sam looked from one to the other. "Can we call it an accord?"

Scarlet didn't want to offer her hand. She raised her glass instead. Ned searched her eyes and raised his own glass. The whiskey burned all the way down.

⌘

They spread out across the surface of the sea, Sam to the center, the others flanking. When sunset came, they remained apart. Scarlet sat on deck for a while, listening to the crew telling stories, then went below to check on her wounded again.

One figure lay in the bunk, in what had once been an officer's cabin and was now the sickbay and home of the *Donnybrook*'s healer. Branna sat up in a hanging canvas chair, as she so often did. Her graying hair picked up red light from the hooded lantern.

"How are they?" Scarlet whispered.

"Patched up. Even Darby's back in his own hammock. He's bled white, and weak as water, but the wound is clean. But young William... Well, see for yourself."

Scarlet shifted forward and looked. Twelve-year-old William lay in the bunk, his blond hair dark with sweat, either asleep or unconscious, moaning with every breath. His left arm lay across his chest, looking as if it had been chewed by a dog. Even in the dim light, Scarlet could see how red and angry the wound looked.

"Will he live?"

"I don't know. I've packed the wound with honey and spider silk. He may yet fight it off."

Scarlet looked at Branna's sad features. "You don't think so."

"If I were a surgeon, I'd take the arm. But you know I have no stomach for that."

"I can ask what help Sam has on the *Bathsheba*."

"I'm brewing one more thing. A charm I've heard of." Branna nodded to a dish on the table. "Mould from bread. If it comes up blue, I'll put it in the wound."

It sounded desperate to Scarlet, but sometimes the strangest magic worked. "I'll pray, too," she offered, and went back to the big aft cabin for her rosary.

At dawn the *Bathsheba* signaled, and they ran on. Scarlet went below and asked after William. "Do I ask Sam's surgeon to come across?"

Branna had heavy circles under both eyes, but her voice was hopeful. "He's fighting back." The cabin was quiet. Scarlet saw blue fuzz in the dish.

"We need to stay together for a while," Scarlet thought. "In case we need that surgeon. I'll give it this day. But I want to haul away from Doyle."

They sighted the schooner as the sun was beginning to slant toward the horizon. She had lost rigging in the storm, and had not bothered to repair it at sea. Bad for her. The three pirate ships formed a net and came in close. Sam fired the warning shot across the schooner's bow just at sunset. The schooner made one last, frantic effort to run, signaling for assistance to someone who probably wasn't there.

Then the *Cardiff Rose* came in and crashed a broadside into the rigging, and the *Donnybrook* cut off all hope of escape, and the schooner spilled the wind from her sails and heaved over obediently.

Scarlet, downwind, began to notice a terrible smell.

Sam was the first onto the Dutch ship. As Scarlet's boarding party came over in the longboat, she saw him talking with the schooner captain. "Is anyone sick onboard?" she demanded, as soon as she was on deck. "There's a foul stench downwind."

Sam turned and jabbered at the captain in Dutch. The man replied but Scarlet could understand none of it.

"He says they have sick passengers below." The man went on, and Sam cocked his head. "I think he's saying it's a very bad sickness. I don't know all the words he's using."

Scarlet looked at the Dutch captain's eyes, and the way he carried his shoulders. "D'ye think, Sam, that he might be lyin' to us?"

"Something's not right. Let's get some lanterns lit."

The pirates lit every candle and lantern they could find. The Dutch crew, probably thirty souls, stood in a quiet mass, and the dim light and silence began to play on Scarlet's nerves. She could hear every lap of waves, every splash of oars as Ned's longboat approached.

Scarlet put a lantern into the hands of a Dutch crewman, and pushed him toward the open hatchway, motioning for him to go below. She followed, pistol in one hand, cutlass loose in her belt. Mister Yeboah came down behind her, Flynn and one of Sam's crewmen following. The smell was worse here, not a smell of sickness, but a back-alley stench of chamber pots and dead rats, old buildings and wet straw.

The crew deck was deserted. Scarlet's boots sounded loud on the deck. She saw captain's and officers' cabins aft, cargo and stores amidships, hammocks for the crew forward, all empty and echoing.

"Sam?" Scarlet called up.

"Yes, Scarlet?"

"Ask the captain where these sick passengers are, for there's not a soul down here."

There was an indistinct murmuring of voices. "He says they're on the orlop deck, below."

Scarlet gritted her teeth. Orlop was the name for a deck below the waterline. The *Donnybrook* kept plunder there, and casks of rum, cannon balls and spare bits of rigging and sails. It was not a place for human beings.

"Sam, could you ask a few more of our people if they'd mind coming down?"

"I'll come." His boots clattered down the ladder.

The hatchway to the orlop was covered by a flap of canvas. When Scarlet pulled it back, the stench of ammonia made her eyes water.

A faint voice came up from below. "*Fóir orainn!*" "*Fóir orainn, le bhur dtoillinn!*"

It was Irish. Cries for help. "My god," whispered Scarlet. "The hold's full of Irish slaves."

For a moment the horror of it caught her up, but then the pitiful, weak voices called her back to herself, and she began to give orders. "Get a ladder. Get Branna off the *Donnybrook*. Open up a cask of water."

Pale light from candles and lanterns revealed dozens of uplifted eyes. The people below were filthy, skeletal. Scarlet offered a few words of encouragement and they scrambled to the open hatchway.

Many were too weak to climb. Yeboah reached down into the dark space, over and over, grasping hands, arms, shoulders, lifting the people up into the fresher air of the crew deck. Finally, forgoing the ladder, he lowered himself into the dark, and began handing bodies up.

Scarlet became aware that someone was calling her name. Sam had her by the arm, and was dragging her toward the upper hatch. She tried to fight her way free of him, to get back to the captives, but he shook her and stared into her eyes.

"Scarlet. Ned's calling. He needs us above." Only then did she hear Doyle's voice. It seemed a hundred leagues away. She stared blindly at Sam, who passed her a cloth. "Here. Wipe your face. The smell of that damned pest-hole has made your eyes water."

Yes. That was it. That was why her cheeks were so wet. She swiped with the cloth, took a deep breath and followed Sam up the ladder. The fresh sea air brought her back to herself. She was able to meet Ned's eyes.

His jaw was rigid as stone. "What the devil's going on down there?"

She set her own face in a blank mask. "The ship's hauling slaves, Ned. Irish slaves. There are scores of them crammed in the orlop deck. Maybe hundreds. I don't know."

Without hesitation, Ned Doyle took four strides to where the Dutch captain stood and beat the man to the deck with three brutal blows. Then he turned back to Sam and Scarlet.

"And is there plague, too, by any chance? Or cholera? Are we all standing here dead, and don't yet know it?" His voice was flat and even, and Scarlet knew by the very lack of emotion how very, very angry the man was.

"I'll be deciding that." Branna lifted her skirts over the railing like a queen, and pushed her way to the open hatch. "And I'll be saying if there's sickness or there's not. Now put up a bit of canvas, and channel some clean air down there. And bring water from our own boats. Clean water and clean air never hurt a soul."

Ned and Scarlet watched her move quietly down the ladder, while Sam picked up the sloop's captain and shook him back to consciousness. There followed another incomprehensible conversation, before Sam threw the man back onto the deck.

"He says an official in London offered him a commission to carry these people to Barbados. He wasn't equipped to carry slaves, but they offered insurance for the voyage, so he figured he'd just write off any that died. He don't know if they're sick or well. He only knows his insurance don't cover pirate attack, and he's pissed that he'll lose money on this run."

At this, something in Scarlet snapped, and she rushed the prone figure, kicking and kicking him over and over, until Sam dragged her off.

She shook herself free and put a hand on her sword. "Get away from me, Sam Bellamy, for angry as I am at this one here, I've also a great wish to be killing Englishmen.

He stepped in close and took her hand. "I'm not an Englishman. I'm a pirate."

"I think," Ned offered, "That it's about time to begin killing Dutch sailors."

Sam spun and looked at him. "What good will that do?"

"Well," drawled Ned, "It wouldn't exactly do good, but it would be a might of vengeance for all them poor souls down below."

"No. They're not all dead. And killing people won't be vengeance. It'll just be slaughter. The sailors in this crew didn't choose their cargo. They're close to slaves themselves. You know how common men live."

"I ain't going to quibble with you. Whatever yon lady tells us as regards whether we're about to contract plague, I don't believe this is a healthy ship. She needs to be burned. And when she is burned, there'll be no place for most of those below."

"What are you saying?" asked Scarlet.

"I'm sayin' that I ain't a hospital ship. I'm a pirate. I can take aboard those that are sailors, or can become sailors, and are of a mind to join my crew. If they're too sick, or too weak, or they're women or children, they're no use to me." He met Scarlet's eyes and touched the edge of his hat. "Present company excluded, darlin'."

Sam stood with his hands on his hips, looking back and forth between the two of them. "I need a drink."

Scarlet shook her head. "You want to get us out of here and get us drunk. I won't do it. I'm moving water casks over here, and whatever else Branna says. Those people deserve to live."

"Well, I'll take this here Dutch feller back to me own ship and talk to him a while." Ned grabbed the schooner's captain by the coat collar and dragged him back in the direction of the boarding ladder. Sam moved to get in the way, but Scarlet caught his sleeve.

"Don't stop him, Sam. They ain't your people."

"Everybody is everybody's people. Slavery's a curse against God."

She laughed and reached up to cup her hand around his rough cheek. "Only to you, dear man. You're some kind of angel. The rest of us are just trying to make it through our days."

Scarlet organized the delivery of water, and such fresh food as the *Donnybrook* had on hand. She watched Ned's first mate, Nick Delacroix, put the trembling Dutch sailors to work, stripping every useful item and bit of brass off the schooner. He put his ferocious smile, white against his midnight skin, with all the teeth filed down to points, to good use. No one did anything stupid. Nick had a cool head, despite his appearance.

All through the night, the pirates picked through bits of the Dutch ship. Piles of rope were set out, barrels of tar, casks of provisions. Ned's men broke open the lockers of the common sailors, carrying clothes, money, and odds and ends onto the moonlit deck.

Sam went through the captain's cabin, taking the logbook for himself, and when Scarlet wasn't moving supplies or arranging for Branna's provisions to be fetched, she helped, picking the lock on the big desk, finding a rather nice dagger hidden under the threadbare pillow, gathering up charts and ink and books.

If she thought about it, she could hear muffled screams coming from the *Rose*. She did her best to shut them out.

She finally put her head down on deck, next to the ship's wheel. Sam woke her with a mug of hot tea, just as dawn was streaking the horizon with pink and blue. "Are we ready to divide the spoils?"

Scarlet scalded her tongue on the tea. "Damn. Where's Ned?"

"Coming over." Sam's mouth was twisted with disgust. "I hope he's washed his hands."

The deck was covered with plunder, but none of it was worth much. Used clothing, bits of the ship, a pitifully small pile of coins. And an enormous problem waited below. Scarlet's back ached. "Do we have any rum for this tea?"

"I left a bottle in the cabin."

Scarlet rose, stretched, and went over to the open hatch. "Branna?"

"Captain."

"We're meeting up here. Best come and tell us what you've found."

"I will."

Sam held the door, then went to sit on the captain's desk. Scarlet sat on the bunk, and was just putting the cork back in the bottle when Ned came in. His hands were clean, but his shirt cuffs, even where he had rolled them back, were crimson. Branna entered a moment later, followed by a man in ill-fitting sailor's clothes. Scarlet guessed from his pallor and sunken cheeks that he was one of the captives.

"God bless all here," Branna said, as if she was entering a home. "This is Father Patrick, come to speak for his people."

Before she had thought about it, Scarlet rose to her feet and dropped a curtsy. It became an opportunity to offer the priest a seat on the bunk, and perch beside Sam, who was staring at her with his jaw slack. Branna sank to the deck, her skirts billowing around her for a moment. Ned leaned against the bulkhead and crossed his ankles, but nodded as well and murmured, "Father."

Scarlet took a sip of fortified tea and asked, "How many alive below?"

"Two hundred and forty-seven," Branna reported. "Starved and weak, suffering terrible from lack of water and air, but no sickness beyond that and festered wounds."

"A large number." Ned glanced at Scarlet and Sam,

"Not nearly so many as set out," the priest replied. "Three hundred and eighty souls in the village, when the English came, and these are the ones left."

Branna looked at Scarlet with speaking eyes. "All the dead are still down there, crammed into the forecastle. It's too dirty to pry them out for burial."

Scarlet put her head into her hands for a moment, then looked back to the priest. "They took your whole village?"

"Every man, woman and child. No reason. The soldiers came, and we were dragged out, leaving all our possessions behind."

Ned picked at something in his teeth. "It's none of our business who profited from it. What matters is, what do we do with them all?"

"Are we still slaves, then?"

"No." Sam's blue eyes met the priest's squarely, though the man quailed a little at the English voice. "But we'll need to burn this ship. We won't throw you into the sea."

"We're grateful, then."

Ned looked at Scarlet. "How many open berths on the *Donnybrook*, darlin'?"

She closed her eyes and moved her fingers. "Twenty-two."

"Um-hum. And you, Mister Bellamy?"

"I can't take more than forty."

"A generous number. A hopeful number. I, myself, can take thirty more men, if they've the stomach to sail with my crew. No molly-coddling."

Scarlet muttered under her breath, "Let's hope it don't come to that."

"Can't you set us ashore somewhere?" Father Patrick's eyes looked hopeful.

"It ain't that easy," Sam explained. "The settlements here are English, Spanish, Portuguese, Dutch and French. The English and the Dutch will have you slaves again, before you can say Jack Robinson. They need workers and they hate Catholics."

"The Spanish and the Portuguese are Catholic," Scarlet added, "but they love to make people slaves, and you don't have the language. I can't see you faring well with them."

Ned nodded. "And the Frenchies run everything in such piss-poor fashion, I wouldn't turn a stray dog over to 'em. Not if it was an Irish dog, at any rate."

Sam drew his legs up under him and sat cross-legged on the desk. "There're so many of you. I'm sure in your own country it's not a large village, but here, it's a settlement. There aren't three thousand souls living in Nassau Port, and that's a big town." Scarlet caught his eye and he shook his head. "I've been figuring all night. Nassau's two-and-a-half weeks away, and every minute of it hard work, dead into the wind. We just can't carry the food and water. And we can't fight with our decks full of civilians. It won't work."

Ned giggled to himself, suddenly. "Well, I got an idea about them Dutch sailors. You want to hear?"

Scarlet was quite sure she did not, but he went on anyway.

"Father Patrick, you say you lost a third of your village. Any of those lost children, by any chance?"

"Too many."

"The mothers of those children, they still alive?"

"Some of them."

"Well then, while we're figuring the rest of Mister Bellamy's plan to set the world straight, why don't we turn them bereaved mothers loose on them Dutch sailors? That'd give us some sport, I bet you!"

"No," Sam said firmly. "The Dutch sailors go into longboats. This ship's and mine."

Ned smiled again. "Thirty men, two longboats. Like to founder. Like to go down."

Sam nodded. "But not certain. One compass between the two. Islands all about. If they make land, they live. Otherwise..."

"You're a fair man, as always, Captain Bellamy. Puttin' it in God's hands."

"In God's hands, Captain Doyle."

Something in what Sam had said rattled in Scarlet's mind. A settlement. She looked up. "I know where we can take these people."

"Where?"

She told them.

Ned barked a laugh. "You must be mad, woman!"

"I am not. There's fruit and pigs in the woods, and a good spring." She turned to Father Patrick. "You have craftsmen? Farmers?"

"We do."

"Just what they need. He'll take you on."

Sam was grinning. "You sure?"

"He's got a heart as soft as spring rain. And if he don't agree, I'll get him drunk and give him what for."

"Fine then. With three ships, it won't be too bad..."

"Two ships," Ned countered. "Two. There's none of these folk I want on my boat. I'm takin' my plunder and heading off."

Sam and Scarlet stared at him.

"I told you, I'm not a hospital. There's goods on the deck. I'll have mine and be off."

There was nothing for it. Sam put the Dutch sailors off in the longboats, as Ned and Nick kicked through the bits of things on deck, picking out what they wanted. Mister Burgess counted the coins into three equal piles. Scarlet oversaw the transport of the captives.

"I hope you don't mind," she told Sam, "but I've settled the good Father in my own cabin. He's promised to say mass tomorrow."

"If it comforts you, Scarlet."

She winked. "I haven't told confession in six months. I reckon this priest will let me off right easy."

They anchored the schooner and got well clear before firing her. The pitch-soaked timber went up in brilliant yellow sheets of flame, so hot it felt like the noon sun. Scarlet heard the priest's words droning on and on, but she added to them in her mind.

"Ready to cast off?" Sam called over, when the hunk was settling into the waves.

"I am." Scarlet replied. "And we have three knots to loose from my Shantyman's magic cord. Be prepared to fly fast, all the way to safe harbor."

They ran on for four days and a half more, as smooth and even as if they had been rolling down a hill. And though he had said many times that he could not control the nature of the wind, the Shantyman may not have been telling the truth. For the *Donnybrook* beat the *Bathsheba* into the cove, and so it was Scarlet who had the privilege of meeting Conner Donnelly on the beach.

"Conner, I've brought you a grand present. You needn't thank me. I'll drop it off and be on my way."

The young man smiled at her, but his eyes were full of questions. "Are you so sure this is something I want?"

"That I am, for I've heard you ask for it many times before. Conner Donnelly, I've brought you a town."

The Bargain

Scarlet called the crew together one more time before entering the port. "Still sure we want to do this?"

Heads nodded all the way around, but expressions were grim.

"We've done our share of good deeds, taking that pack of slaves in and setting 'em up with the Donnellys on shore. Shouldn't we be off filling our hold with treasure? Why are we mucking about here?"

Darby spoke up. "We ain't never had a chance before to buy our own people on the slave block, before they're sold to the rich folk. It's like a sign. We ought to do it."

Scarlet sighed to herself and rejoined. "We ain't had a proper job in over a month. Our hold is down to odds and ends, and there's no profit before us. Conner made his share of profit, cutting a deal to take them refugees off our hands. Ain't it time we pulled in a little gold ourselves?"

No one flinched or argued. Scarlet looked around the deck, meeting eyes. When she got to Flynn, he gave her a grim smile and said, "We're an Irish ship, Cap'n. It's Irish business. We don't mind doing it."

Scarlet looked at Mister Yeboah, Sanchez, William, Pryce. "We ain't all Irish."

"Some of us want to be," piped young William.

The crew laughed, and Scarlet stepped forward and ruffled his blonde curls. "You don't, boy. An Irish orphan would never have lived to this ripe old age."

William sulked, and Scarlet shook her head. "As you will. I'll do as you will. I'll grant, it's odd to go into a tavern and learn of a shipload of our countrymen being sold like cattle. Maybe it is a sign. At any rate, you outvote me. How much do we spend?"

"All of it!" someone yelled, and others took it up.

Scarlet turned to her quartermaster. "Burgess, they say everything in the chest. What say you?"

Burgess thumbed through his book as he stepped forward. "We cannot bankrupt the ship. We need our usual hundred pounds for supplies and emergencies. And it's not wise," here he looked over his glasses at Scarlet, "to be without coins in our pockets. That said, we should reasonably be able to purchase forty people, assuming the Frenchies are willing to turn them over to us."

"How'd you come up with that figure?"

"Five pounds a slave. That's what they sell for in Martinique. Beyond what I've mentioned, the common lot of treasure comes to two hundred pounds."

Scarlet shook her head. "That's only if we can catch the lot on auction day. If they've already been sold off, we must offer more, to rouse them t' do as we want. And if we're dealing with slave-owners, we must also offer a gift. It always warms up negotiations."

Burgess raised his eyebrows. "We could certainly offer them damned elephant teeth. I told you not to take them."

"No, them things mark us as pirates or smugglers. What gems do we have?"

99

Burgess flipped several pages and muttered under his breath. "Let me see... ah, here it is. Fourteen odd pieces of jewelry, nine with stones. We gave the gold earrings off those Dutch sailors to the Donnellys."

"Anything flashy?"

"None that I remember." Burgess looked thoughtful. "What a shame we no longer have that ruby necklace Governor Avery lent you."

"No shame at all. Some things ain't worth the trouble they cause. What else have we got? What's respectable?"

Burgess paged through a bit more. "Here it is. Most respectable item on the ship. The Holy Bible, in Latin. Red leather binding, silver trim, mahogany storage box. Picked it up nine months ago."

"Just the item! Two hundred pounds, and a Bible. Well, we'll see if we can just buy these folk and head out to sea again, or if we'll have to rescue them some other way. I'm in, for good or ill. Mister Pryce, set us a course for the port of Fort-de-France on Martinique."

⌘

Captain Robert Davenport of the *Nightingale* sat at table in the grand stateroom of the India Trader *Boulder,* keeping his back straight and his face correctly interested, while his host rattled on about the difficulties involved in importing tea.

"...is enough to make a man feel his work is unappreciated."

"I'm certain you receive great consolation from your commitment to the company."

The table before them was dotted with exotic dishes in a display which better conveyed novelty than hospitality. Robert would have much preferred plain boiled beef, but he was embroiled in politics.

His host, Herbert Stille, inhabited the grand aft cabin of the trading ship, a place usually reserved for the ship's captain, and he occupied it in grand style. Had it not been for the creaking of the timbers and the beams above his head, Robert could have believed himself in an English drawing room. They had traveled together from London, and had visited between ships often enough that, had Stille been a different man, Robert might have considered him a friend.

There had been finger bowls with the meat course. Finger bowls indeed! After nearly twenty years in the Navy, where fresh water was severely rationed for officers and men alike, squandering it on such fripperies felt like an insult to all the sailors who had ever died of thirst.

Robert remembered his mission and found it in himself to smile. "We should be coming up on Fort-de-France around midnight. I've spent so long fighting the French it seems odd to be this close without the guns run out."

Stille ran his plump fingers over his own vast silk waistcoat. "I thought you'd just come over."

"Two months ago. I fought the French in the Mediterranean. Have you decided? Will you stop at Fort-de-France first, or tarry in Saint-Pierre?"

"Fort-de-France. We can go in first thing in the morning."

Robert bit back a sarcastic remark about the Royal Navy having its timetables set by the East India Trading Company. Instead he offered, "Considering how many warships your company employs, I'm surprised you requested the *Nightingale*'s escort."

Stille smiled to himself and leaned back. "It adds an air of respectability. Some of these hereditary nobles don't think well of a self-made man."

Robert gestured toward the Madera, and Stille refilled both the glasses. "I don't understand why you believe the French will allow you a monopoly on trade with them."

"Because their own trading company, the '*Compagnie de Indes Occidentales*', has gone bankrupt. Mine is the richest in the world. They need slaves to run the island. I can supply the slaves. It's as simple as that."

"But will they trust you? Three years ago we were at war."

"Yes. And we may be again, in a year or two. In the meantime, the Company will grow in influence, and perhaps help to control the politics of the future."

Robert had been only distantly aware how much political affairs would come to play in his new assignment. It was certainly the part he found least appealing. "Well, let us hope our time on Martinique is profitably spent."

⌘

The *Donnybrook* did not usually sail by night, but they were trying to beat a slave ship into port, so several hands had volunteered to stay up and pilot. Scarlet paced, fretting about the risk and the time wasted, all because Flynn had heard about this shipment of slaves while gossiping in a dockside bar.

A little after sunset she shut herself in her cabin to lay out a suitable wardrobe and think about how to maneuver the deal. The lantern-light shown on silks, satins and velvet, for she believed a pirate captain should dress the part.

Some crewmember tapped on the door. She did not bother to look, just said, "Enter." Should she choose the red skirt, she wondered, or the cream colored one?

"Ma'am?" the boy's voice caught her attention. She turned and put her hands on her hips.

"William. Shouldn't you be in your hammock?"

He raised his chin with an admirable stubbornness. "I ain't a child."

"You will be 'til your voice changes."

They frowned at each other while William thought. Finally he added, "I'm still a member of the crew, so it's my right to come here."

"Oh, so it's business. Well, then. Sit." Scarlet offered him a chair, and took her own seat behind the captain's desk. "What do you want, young William?"

"I can count, same as anyone. And I was with you when you bought Mister Yeboah. You paid fifty pound for 'im. And now Mister Burgess says a slave ain't worth but five. Did you squander the ship's money?"

Scarlet felt a great sadness come over her heart, but she looked at William evenly. "I did no such thing. The issue is that Mister Yeboah is an African, and the slaves we are going to buy are Irish."

William worked it through. "The Africans are worth so much more?"

"They are. The Africans must be bought, from the folk in their own country what make them slaves. The Irish are herded up by the English army, and they have no value except the cost of transport. They – we – are worked to death accordingly."

He thought again. "Why do the English do it?"

Tears stung at the back of Scarlet's eyes, but she held them back, and kept her face still. "Because we are Catholic and of a different mind from the English folk. An English Protestant named Cromwell decided sixty years ago that the Irish race must be killed off entire."

"That's…" Williams' eyes wandered around the cabin, looking for an answer. "That's wrong."

"It is. I believe it is. That's part of why I turned pirate. But it's the way of the world, young William. Do you see now why so

103

many of the folk you meet on these pirate ships are Irish? Do you wonder that so many of us are angry?"

"You ain't angry at English folk. You took me in. And my mother was born in England."

"You were a likely lad," Scarlet said, remembering the scrawny child who had tried to pick her pocket, and then to talk his way out of a beating. "I could have done much worse."

"What will happen to the slaves we buy?"

"We will free them, young William, and take them to Donnelly's Cove, where, God help us, Conner Donnelly will take them to live free, and not strip the brass off our ship in payment. Mary's Grace, let it be so."

⌘

Robert stood before the looking-glass in his cabin aboard the *Nightingale* and checked his appearance one more time before joining Stille on shore. White horsehair wig, carefully curled and perfectly in place, black, tri-cornered hat square on top of it, shirt starched to within an inch of life itself, the high collar and stiff neck-cloth utterly correct and almost unbearably tight. The long buff waistcoat, gold trimmed, was tightly buttoned, except for the top two, which served the function of displaying the neck-cloth to advantage.

Navy blue wool coat, the lightest weight available but still uncomfortable in the Caribbean climate, also gold trimmed, this time in lace worth six months of his pay. At least the breeches could be plain, with only gold buttons at the knee. His hose, silk, were not nearly as comfortable as knitted cotton, but considerably more fashionable, at least according to his London tailor.

The buckles on his black shoes concerned him. He did not like to carry debt, and unless war broke out or he had uncommonly good luck hunting pirates, it would require three months of further payments to complete the purchase of the gold buckles. Nevertheless, the weight of solid gold was reassuring. No matter what inadequacies he showed as an ambassador, he could at least be assured of giving the proper appearance.

A wild assortment of buildings, bright in tropical shades of yellow green and blue were dug into the volcanic cliffs above the port, like birds' nests, and the dark stone fort loomed grimly. But the piers and docks teemed with commerce, a regular crush of slaves, sailors, merchants, and women, all simultaneously hauling, calling, carrying and trading. Packs of dogs and children dodged through the crowd.

Stille waved a lace-and-linen handkerchief. "Here!" he called. His embroidered silk suit looked considerably more comfortable than Robert' attire, though the extravagant curls of his periwig must surely be hot. "There you are. I've been given the names of several prominent men in town who may further my cause. Townhouses mostly. Would you care to walk, or d'you think we should engage a carriage?"

"If we walk, you'd best watch your pockets"

Robert led the way out of the crush and toward several carriages waiting along a nearby street. He was just raising an arm to hail one of the drivers when a man stepped out of the way, and he spotted the back of a very familiar head of red hair.

Without waiting to see if Stille kept up with him, Robert shouldered two people out of the way and bore down on the red-haired woman. When he was close enough to touch her, he bellowed, "Scarlet MacGrath" in his most authoritative voice.

The woman spun toward him, eyes wide in a brief flash of fear, and Robert saw that it was indeed the pirate. He reached for her and said firmly, "You are under arrest."

The girl evaded him with a few nimble steps, but did not flee. Instead she raised her chin and answered, "I am not."

Her reply was so surprising that he was brought up short. "What do you mean?"

The chin went up higher still, and the green eyes flashed. "I mean that we ain't in English waters, Bobby, and you have no authority here."

A fact. An undeniable fact. Robert felt rage fighting with exasperation. "I will alert the port authority. You'll be arrested by the French marines."

"I will not." Those eyes met his in a way no woman's ever had before, measuring and triumphant, and her lips curved in a smile. "You never read all your dispatches, or else the English never knew. I've yet to rob a French ship. I ain't a pirate here."

They stood in the street, glaring at each other. Robert wished for some reason, that he was confronting her while wearing his regular uniform and not his dress blues. Her own costume was outlandish in the extreme. She wore a man's hat over her long red tresses, a red jacket cut off short at the hip, and an intricate red brocade skirt, looped up to the knees. Although Robert knew he shouldn't, he could not escape glancing below the skirt, only to see a pair of Frenchmen's boots, tight and curved and decorated with high red heels.

That had been a mistake. She laughed at him, then turned her body and looked over her shoulder like a coquette. "Like what you see, Bobby? Then you should come over; I give it to pirates." She spun on one of those elaborate red heels and stalked off, flaunting her hips.

⌘

"Sweet Jesus. Sweet Jesus. Sweet Jesus." Flynn tagged along at Scarlet's side, still carrying the Bible, nearly weeping with terror. "I ain't never seen such a thing in my life. You and the rodgering Royal bastard Navy having it out in the very street. Sweet Jesus."

"Shut it," Scarlet replied. She could hardly believe she'd gotten away with such a ploy. Her hands and face were still cold, and the pit of her stomach roiled. "I knew what I was about."

"How could you? How could anybody?"

"It's a neutral port for us. What, you think I didn't know that? You think I didn't figure it in when the fool officers come to me with this fool plan? I don't run about trading with the authorities unless I know I ain't about to be arrested."

"He could still have nabbed you."

Scarlet paused. "Not that one." She glanced back down the street. "That one's honorable." Her searching eyes found nothing. The Navy officer was gone.

⌘

"What the devil was that about?"

Robert took a deep breath, wishing he could hide the color rising to his cheeks, and stepped into the shade between two buildings. "That woman is a pirate."

"What?" Stille craned his neck back toward the street to see. "A pirate's wench?"

"No. A pirate. The captain of the *Donnybrook*. I didn't believe it myself, at first. We have records of her going back three years."

"Then why didn't you arrest her?"

Robert gave a grim smile. "Because this is a French port. I don't have the authority."

Stille sputtered. "That hardly signifies. A woman, out in the street? It would've been the simplest thing in the world to seize her and carry her back to the *Nightingale*."

"Simple, perhaps, but not legal."

"What the devil does that matter?"

Robert looked into Stille's eyes. "The law matters very much. It's the only thing holding civilization together. Without it, we're savages, apes in the trees. It is my place to uphold the law, Mister Stille, and you might be wise to remember it."

⌘

Scarlet found the slave market by asking directions of a man on the street, and came up to a rough walled courtyard, fitted with pens and a raised platform. The place stood empty except for a man with carpentry tools, tinkering with the latch on one of the pens. She questioned him in her bad French while Flynn strolled about, looking at posters along the walls which showed Africans and what appeared to be very downcast French peasants.

"They sell their own?" Flynn asked, pointing, as Scarlet finished her discussion and handed over a silver coin.

"If there are poor people in France, then they likely do. We lot always get the short end of everything. I'll tell you, Flynn, we've lost our men. The lot of Irish was sold off a week ago. They're likely dying of sunburn in some cursed cane field. Let's get back to the ship."

Flynn drew his eyebrows together. "That's too easy, Captain. You ain't really in this with us, or you'd not give up so soon. What's the matter? You were pleased to make a home for the last lot."

Scarlet sighed and stared down at the road. "I'm thinkin' of the *Donny* and my own crew, and that bloody great warship in the harbor. The odds of this working out get worse by the minute. I don't like it. Let's get out."

"It ain't proved. Don't give up 'til it's proved, Captain." Flynn stepped in front of her and caught her eyes with an earnest look. "You're lucky, Captain. Your folk were killed in Ireland. My da' was transported, and I never knew what happened to him. I saw the slaves on that damned Dutch ship, and I felt I was lookin' on family. You've already foxed this Navy man. Give us your best."

108

Scarlet nodded slowly. "I didn't know about your da'. All right. This fellow says there's a man with a fine house on the hill what has bought a great number of slaves. He might be worth talkin' to."

"Shall we find a carriage for hire?"

"Best so, for we'll never find the place elsewise. Man's named Monsieur Charles de Bellecombe."

They found a carriage and gave the name. The driver seemed impressed.

⌘

Stille continued to sputter and swear as Robert hailed a carriage and opened the door. Robert took a deep breath and let him go on for a moment, then cut in. "You have something in mind with these social visits?"

The subject back on himself, Stille became more congenial. "My company's proposition, by itself, is a benefit to the country. But, introduced by a valued French citizen, it has considerably more substance. I have letters of introduction. I will make the acquaintance of these gentlemen, present my case, and gain their support."

"And my purpose in being present is to hint at the approval of the government?"

"Exactly."

Robert hid his sigh of dismay. He did not look forward to being idle, but it seemed that his duty for the next several hours was to be decorative, which struck him as being worse. His eyes slid to the fort looming over the harbor, and he counted cannons. At least he could do some reconnaissance while being dragged on this social round.

⌘

Scarlet watched out the window, noting locations and memorizing the route as the driver rolled them up the hill, through a rat's warren of streets, grand tall houses rising from between more humble homes, vendors of fruit and flowers working from push-carts in the streets.

The only fault that she could find in the place was that it seemed thinly populated. Some of the great houses stood empty, and away from the bustle of the port, the streets were nearly bare.

The carriage pulled up before a pale yellow home with arched windows and a deep porch. Scarlet spoke to the carriage driver until he understood that he needed to wait for her, then tipped him extravagantly.

She rang the bell, feeling the rush in her veins coming up, just as it did when she held a pistol to a man's head, or the *Donnybrook* went into battle. Beside her, Flynn licked his lips and asked, "Do we give him the Bible straight off?"

"Wait until I set in to deal. I'll signal."

A porter answered the door and Scarlet did her best to look down her nose and act like someone who visited houses like this every day. She pronounced the name, and gave her own as if it meant something. The porter looked her up and down, noted the hired carriage, saw Flynn and that he was carrying something, and ushered them into a room to wait.

When the servant returned Scarlet, with Flynn following, was taken to a sort of office, full of graceful gilded furniture. The man seated behind the ornamented desk was dressed in an apple-green suit and full wig.

Scarlet gave a formal bow, doffing her hat and extending a leg. Monsieur de Bellecombe seemed to appreciate the leg, and Scarlet gave him one of her warmest smiles. He was older, and possessed the largest nose she had ever seen, but managed to be attractive despite it.

Scarlet stumbled her way through a few pleasantries, and then Bellecombe asked if she would rather proceed in English.

"Thank you, milord. I have this language better."

"Mine is not so good, but better than your French, perhaps?"

"I'm sure of it, sir. I've come on business, but hope it will be a profit to us both."

His smile was frank, but not businesslike. "What commerce could such a beautiful young woman possibly be engaged in?"

"A serious one, milord." Scarlet took a deep breath and put on a suitably serious face. "I've come to speak of your immortal soul."

A smile crinkled the corners of his eyes. "This cannot be. You hardly appear to be a nun!"

"I am a good Catholic, sure, and I fear for the souls of my fellows. I have learned that, ten days ago, some of my countrymen was brought to this place by the bloody English, and been sold into slavery. They are good Catholics, sir, and it's against the laws of God that one Catholic should own another."

The man stopped smiling, and made a church of his fingers. Scarlet reckoned he was thinking about money. She went on.

"A group of us has joined together, and raised two hundred pounds to buy back our fellows. After all, it ain't proper that a man should lose money over doing what's right. We offer to pay you, and any of your friends what own these Catholic slaves, a fair price for any as can be found and turned over."

The mention of two hundred pounds raised the temperature in the room back up where it should be. Monsieur de Bellecombe apparently had a high regard for females who wore their skirts pinned up to the knee, and also spoke so lightly about a sum of money equal to what a sugar plantation might make in half a year.

"You understand that I do not go to these sales myself, though I know my estate manager has bought slaves lately. But of course, I will do everything in my power to aid you."

"That would be kind, sir." The man seemed sincere, and not the least put off by her appearance or her offer. Scarlet beckoned, and Flynn stepped forward, holding out the ornamented box. "Will you please accept this gift? The words of God, for a man who understands their importance."

From the way the man's eyes lit up when he opened the box, the book inside must have been quite a treasure. Bellecombe seemed suddenly stricken with good fellowship. "And I have not even offered you a glass of wine!" He called into the next room "Dufour! Bring refreshments for my guest."

Scarlet murmured that perhaps she should not stay.

"Ah, but I insist. Stay with me, and I will send out messages at once to my estates. You may have your answer by this evening."

"Then I'd be pleased to do it. The climate here ain't easy on folk from my country. They don't last well in the heat and the sun. It would be a pleasure to get them home safe."

Bellecombe set a chair out with his own hand. "Keep me company while I write, and afterwards I will show you the garden."

Scarlet sat, showing her boots off to good advantage. "And will your lady wife be joinin' us?"

"Alas, Mademoiselle, I am a widower."

"How very sad."

An hour later a messenger had been sent out, and Scarlet was walking through a flower garden, arm in arm with the French gentleman, and Flynn was cooling his heels with Bellecombe's servants. Scarlet sincerely hoped he was making inroads with the housemaids, for she was having a lovely time.

"...and over there is the rose arbor. A lovely place; we should go and sit."

Scarlet pouted and put a resisting hand on his chest. "It's out o' sight of the house, Monsieur de Bellecombe. The servants would talk." Pleasant company as the man was, she did not intend to give him what he wanted until she had some Irish slaves safe on the *Donnybrook*'s crew deck.

"Please, you must call me Charles."

"And you may call me Scarlet. But I ain't going into no rose arbors yet."

"You devastate me, Mademoiselle."

She leaned in and put her lips very close to his ear. "I have business. Business comes first."

He smiled, and took a polite step backward, keeping his eyes warm. "But, Mademoiselle, I have business as well."

Scarlet did her best to imitate a Frenchwoman's one-shouldered shrug.

"It is not impossible, Mademoiselle, that you have some knowledge of pirates." He held up a finger. "Now, it so happens that I have dealt with French privateers, and my dealings have been most entertaining. Perhaps together we could find a method to acquaint my business managers with people who may be trying to sell unusual objects?"

"That would please me right fine. As it happens, I do know of some 'unusual objects' that're wanting for a home. But as I've said, my business with these slaves comes first. When we've done that deal we can speak of the rest." She smiled and picked an imaginary bit of lint off his coat. "All the rest."

"Tell me, Mademoiselle Scarlet, what are these people to you? Why have you really come to get them? I think you must have a very good reason."

Scarlet studied the fine white gravel under her toes, then turned and began to walk. The crew had dragged her into this. She did not like thinking about the horrors of the lower deck of a slave ship, or the pathetic gratitude of the Irish folk who had survived long enough to be set free. The memory of it called her to the whisky bottle. It kept her up at night, listening to the *Donnybrook* moving around her. It made her wonder if Sam Bellamy was right, if pirates might have a higher purpose than living a brief, violent, free life.

The Frenchman matched her steps. "I regret my question. It has caused you pain, and that was not my intent. Has the mademoiselle lost someone?"

Scarlet found her smile and put it back on. "All of us lose folk in this life. If you're askin', there's no lover of mine amongst these slaves. My reasons are as I've told you."

He took her arm again and patted her hand. "Well, we must get these countrymen of yours into your hands as soon as possible. As it happens, I have friends coming tonight. You must stay, and become acquainted with them. They own plantations, and purchase slaves. A generous offer will move them. As well as the sight of a pretty girl. Have you a dress that you can send for? It is a bit formal, this party."

"I'll send my man back for it. This is very kind of you, Monsieur."

"I have hopes of a long and pleasant acquaintance, Mademoiselle Scarlet."

The smile on her face felt more comfortable now. "As do I."

⌘

Robert stood in the welcome shade of the townhouse's spreading porch, listening with half an ear as Stille offered polite French introductions and engraved visiting cards to the house's liveried servant. From this position, high on the hill, he could see the layout of the port, the encircling harbor, and the stern block of the stone fort.

Without understanding the French, his ear caught an invitation to enter the home, and his attention snapped back in time to remove his hat and follow Stille into the house.

The décor in this place captured Robert's attention at once. Instead of paintings, the sitting room was decorated with flat wood carvings, apparently African. A box on the side table flashed with tiny inset mirrors, in the Indian fashion. The rug was Moroccan. Robert knew that trade brought all sorts of things to the European colonies, but these items did not seem the usual commercial items. He had the impression of mementoes, souvenirs, trophies.

The master of the house entered, laughing and calling to someone in another room. From his fashionable periwig to his fashionable high-heeled shoes, he was dressed entirely in black, down to the affectation of black shirt and hose. A diamond stud flashed from one earlobe. He exchanged florid gestures and a wordy greeting with Stille, then turned to Robert.

"*Capitaine* Davenport, is it not? The commander of the frigate the English have sent over?"

Robert nodded curtly. "I have that honor. Robert Davenport, of the *Nightengale*. But I'm sorry, sir, Mister Stille has not made me aware of your name."

"*Capitaine* Jacques Tavernier. Of the *Achille*." Tavernier exchanged bows with Robert, then spoke again at length with Stille, seeming to take offense that he had not been properly introduced. Robert watched them closely.

He recalled the name Tavernier. Not a French Navy captain, but a privateer. The luxurious home suddenly made much more sense. What was not so clear was why Stille wanted to speak to the man. Privateers operated, legally, in time of war. France had not been at war with anyone for over two years.

Bare feet pattered on the hardwood floor, a half-naked toddler came dashing into the room, giggling and shrieking. Immediately after him came a pretty young lady, laughing almost

115

too hard to stand. The toddler raced around Robert's knees, until Tavernier scooped the child up and swung him high, laughing again. Then the young woman advanced, blushing and bowing before her husband's guests. She took the toddler in her arms and backed away with a smile and lowered eyes.

Tavernier turned back to Stille and Robert. "Please excuse my son. He is too little for manners. I am most pleased that you have come, but I have little time." He gestured to his own extravagant clothes. "I was just leaving for some visits, and afterwards I have an engagement for dinner."

"We are devastated to inconvenience you," Stille replied, then added something in French. Robert watched as Tavernier's face clouded and Stille's eyebrows drew together. Stille had some leverage against the man. Interesting.

The two men fenced verbally for a few moments. Robert would have given much to know what they were saying, but he kept alert, watching the faces. It occurred to him that more was going on here than socializing in pursuit of trade. He wondered if he could trust his own distaste of Stille.

Tavernier looked from Robert to Stille and back. Finally he raised a hand with a flourish. "Ah! But I have a marvelous idea. Why do you not accompany me to dinner? I am sure you would be most welcome."

"I would not dream of such an imposition," Robert protested, just as Stille said, "We would be delighted." For a moment they stood in silence. Robert realized that, strange though the situation was, it was his best chance to learn more about the goings on. He raised a hand in acquiescence. "If you both believe we would be welcome, how can I argue?"

Tavernier glanced sharply at Stille, and smiled. "Let me write something for you. The address and the gentleman's name. He stepped away, came back blowing a piece of paper, and handed it to Stille.

116

Back in the carriage, Robert glared at Stille and demanded, "What are you thinking?"

"A most satisfactory introduction to dine with a number of influential gentlemen."

Robert considered his answer. "I'm no diplomat. But unless I misremember every lesson I ever learned as a boy, there is no worse behavior than to appear unannounced at a dinner party."

Stille laughed genially. "I take your point. But this is not a seated dinner party. It will be a cold buffet. Very French. We should both have an amusing time tonight, and I should make some fine contacts as well."

⌘

Flynn came up from the servant's quarters with his hair mussed. "Ah, Captain Scarlet, I knew you had it in you. How's it going with the grand gentleman above?"

"Mighty fine above, and how goes it in the servant's hall?"

"Grand. I was even recruiting."

"Recruiting?"

"Recruiting, sure. I've just about got this French girl persuaded to marry me. She'll be a fine addition to the crew."

"And you without any of the French language."

"And me pickin' it up at a rapid rate."

"You can have another go at her later. Now you need to heel off back to the ship and get Pryce. Tell 'er I need a grand dress, and the full rig that comes with it. The very best thing we have lyin' about the ship. I'm meeting a room full of rich men tonight, and I need to look like a bloody duchess.

Flynn looked worried, but Scarlet poked him in the chest and went on. "And tell Mister Burgess to get ready for a trading session. I think I've found us a fence for them elephant teeth, and them bolts of silk, and all them bloody teapots. We may even end up trading for the slaves."

117

"Praise all the saints. But can't you write a note and send it with one of the Frenchie's servants? I don't like to leave you alone here."

"That can't be helped. It'd take me an hour to write it all down. You'll move quicker and tell better. Go ahead, take the carriage. And make sure the carriage waits at the ship, so Pryce rides back in it."

⌘

Robert boarded his ship in a foul temper, stalked past the sideboys hastily assembled to pipe him aboard. He took a quick report from the first lieutenant and flung himself into the big aft cabin, calling for his steward.

"Yes, sir." A stiff posture, a crisp salute. Hughes knew how to deal with his captain when Robert was put out. He took Robert's coat and hung it up to air, and immediately went to the chest for a clean shirt. Robert sighed. He was being managed, and managed quite well. It was unfair to put Hughes on his mettle over something so trivial.

Robert untied his neck cloth and sat. "You may stand down, Hughes. I have no intention of sending a broadside your way."

"As you say, sir." Hughes' back remained ramrod-straight, but a smile came into his eyes. He held out the shirt.

"No, I'm sorry. I need to wash and dress for a dinner party at eight."

Hughes paused. "A dinner party, sir?"

"Yes, something French called a 'buffet'. I don't suppose you know the etiquette of the thing?"

"I shall make inquiries, sir."

Robert had no idea where Hughes made his inquires, but whatever sources he consulted, the results had always been remarkably useful. He'd have something besides Stille's dubious advice to guide him. The prospect of the upcoming dinner lost some of its dread. Robert peeled off his damp dress-shirt and tossed it onto the bunk, and watched Hughes get out the basin and the wash-stand.

⌘

Scarlet sat at a card table in the drawing room, teaching Charles to play "maw" when a servant came and whispered something. Bellecombe sighed mightily and put down his cards. "I have been rescued. There are no rules to this game. You are making them up!"

"There are rules galore," Scarlet replied, giving him a mischievous smile, "But the first rule is that I'm only allowed to tell you the first rule, and that's this one."

Bellecombe threw his hands into the air, just as a woman in a neat maid's uniform entered, carrying a large, flat box. Scarlet stared at her in surprise for a moment, until the maid winked and she recognized Pryce.

"Would milady care to examine these things?"

Scarlet would have said "no," but Pryce's expression told her something. She rose from the table and smiled into Bellecombe's eyes. "Is there a place where I can go with my maid?"

Five minutes later, she and Pryce were in a slightly dusty woman's bedchamber. Pryce plopped the box down and began unwinding a length of fabric. Scarlet stared at it in wonder. "You can't expect me to tell you if it's right or not? I don't even know what it is."

"I expect you to start getting into this. It's a dinner party, right?"

"So I'm told."

"You need to put all this on, and I need to do your hair. We'd best hope there's some cosmetics I can borrow, for we had none. You're lucky I was saving this out. It's too big in the bust for

119

me, but it should fit you fine. The rest we'll do with lacing." She put her hands on her hips. "Well? Take off your clothes. We need to get started."

"The man said the guests was expected at eight.

"That's right. It's after five now. There's not a moment to waste."

⌘

"I look like a bleeding figurehead."

Scarlet stood before the long looking-glass, hands held out to her sides, staring at the stranger who looked back at her. Pryce had scrubbed her unmercifully, powdered her, pinched her into a pair of stays until she could hardly breathe, draped her in a dozen yards of fabric, powdered her again, painted her lips and cheeks, then spent an hour pulling her hair. The last step had involved sewing her into the dress. Scarlet felt that movement, any movement, was near impossible. But she did look like a duchess.

Her long red hair had been teased into a towering construction, slicked and cemented with scented grease, then curled with a hot iron. The curls hung over her bare shoulder.

Scarlet's shoulders and bosom had never been so exposed, short of the bedchamber, and the sight of her own flesh, powdered pale and on blatant display, was near to make her blush. With every breath, her exposed breasts strained at the scanty fabric of the dark blue bodice, for the murderous stays prevented her from breathing as she was used to, from her belly. Her body was confined in a conical tube of canvas, stiffened with wooden strips, rigid as a corpse.

The dress's spreading skirts were a wonder of construction. Where the stays kept her rigid, the skirts gave her grace. The many yards of fabric draped artfully, and would have been too long, had not Pryce provided a pair of high-heeled shoes. The shoes, mercifully, were no taller than Scarlet's French boots, but the toes pinched.

"Can we hide a brace of pistols under this rig? Or at least a knife or two?"

"You don't need 'em Captain. You have all the weapons you need." Pryce nodded at Scarlet's bodice.

"How's that?"

"Hold your shoulders back. Now look at yourself." Scarlet examined her reflection, and Pryce went on. "When a man looks at those, you know what he's thinking? He's thinking nothing at all, and that's just what you want from 'em. That was the first thing I learned when I was fifteen, and come out in Society."

For twenty minutes Pryce schooled her in how to walk and turn, and manage a fan, and then the maid came up and asked if she was ready to come down to the buffet. Scarlet begged a moment, and the maid withdrew.

"There you go." Pryce looked at her with a mixture of analysis and affection. "It's no use to ask you to be anyone but yourself. You couldn't do it. You look right fine, though. More a queen, I'd say, then a duchess. I met a duchess once, and she was awfully stiff. Oh, I almost forgot."

She dug into a pocket. "Here. You should wear emeralds, they'd set off your eyes, but pearls were all we had."

Scarlet took out her gold earrings, replaced them with pearl pendants, and draped three ropes of pearls around her neck. Then she went down to the buffet, whatever in the name of God that was.

⌘

Tavernier had sent his carriage down, and the coachman came to the *Nightingale* at a mere quarter until the hour of eight.

Robert was pacing, pulling at his vest buttons. Just like a Frenchman to be late.

He still had a dreadful sinking feeling about the manners involved in being invited by a third party to dinner, and the thought that it was Stille's error, not his own, did little to help his nerves. He did not want to be made a fool, especially in front of the damned French. Only deep suspicion of what Stille was up to kept him from manufacturing some excuse to remain with the ship.

Tavernier's carriage, like Tavernier's home, and Tavernier's blushing wife, were enviable. Robert knew of English naval captains who had made fortunes, collecting their rewards for captured ships, but he had never seen it personally. This close, it was dazzling. The carriage was made of shining coffee-brown wood, trimmed with silver and pulled by a team of horses whose color matched the carriage perfectly.

The cooler air of evening made Robert's dress coat much more bearable, and Stille had used this event as an excuse to put on a suit so magnificent he looked as if he belonged at the royal court.

The coachman sat stiffly in his seat, the footman held the carriage door correctly. But Tavernier was not inside. Robert looked at Stille.

Stille cocked an eyebrow. "Perhaps he has chosen to walk?"

Robert could only hope they were not somehow being played with.

Seated in the coach's plush interior, Robert held his hands deliberately still and thought about the lovely woman and her beautiful child. And the French privateer, owner of his ship and free to stay on land if he wished. Robert was thirty two, and had been at sea for nearly twenty years. Loneliness dragged at him like a weight. He could only hope that the Caribbean would treat him as kindly as it had Tavernier.

The horses strained up the hill, and Robert looked out into the dark. Most of the houses they passed had lanterns beside their doors, but the light from the carriage's running lamps threw leaping shadows over hedges and walkways. Robert looked out toward the fort, but couldn't see its outline along the side of the hill. Odd, they did not seem to be using the same route the hired carriage had taken earlier.

They stopped before a two story townhouse and the footman went to the door. A moment later Tavernier stepped out, leading a young lady. Robert and Stille emerged from the carriage to bow her in, but flickering lanterns revealed a woman of different features entirely, black hair and skin that hinted at the deep tones of a native. As she passed him by, her eyelashes fluttered and she smiled invitingly.

Tavernier smiled, waved a scented handkerchief, and presented Stille and Robert to his companion, then switched easily to English and introduced her as "My dear friend *Madame* Ave."

No pretense, even, that she was respectable. Stille bowed, as if to a decent woman, and Robert consented to nod. He had it only by rumor, but courtesans of the highest rank were accorded the title due a married lady. Tavernier handled her like a lady, but his eyes twinkled.

Robert watched the privateer and his second beautiful lady, and felt his hands curling into fists.

With everyone seated, the carriage rolled on.

⌘

Scarlet came down the stairs and met Bellecombe, feeling naked as a plucked goose. His eyes were warm, and he kissed her hands. She managed to remain cool and keep her mouth curled in an amused smile.

He brought her into the withdrawing room, where a trio of musicians played artful music. Bellecombe walked her about, showing her a table full of elaborate food (plates on one side, laid just the same as a party on the *Donnybrook*). "Will you stand by me as I receive my guests?" he asked.

So when the first knock came at the door, and the servant went to answer, Scarlet stood at Bellecombe's left hand, and heard him say "*Capitaine* MacGrath? May I present *Monsieur* Galland? And his companion, *Madame* Labelle." Scarlet noted that the lady was his "companion," and listened sharp to the French introduction. She heard "*Capitaine*" next to her name, as was proper, and *Donnybrook*. She bowed to the man, difficult in the dress, and reached for the woman's hand. It was so white and soft that for a moment she wanted to hide her own scarred, calloused fingers.

But this woman was a companion, not a wife, and certainly not the captain of a ship of twelve guns. Scarlet clasped the woman's hand as if she were a friend. The girl looked at her with sharp eyes. Scarlet smiled.

More guests came in. Scarlet heard many French names, noted how each man looked at her, and heard herself introduced as a ship's captain and "acquirer of rare things". Her hand was kissed over and over, and eyes strayed as Pryce had thought they would. Scarlet realized that these fellows thought they would have an advantage against her in a trade. They had never seen her with a pistol in her hand, and thought her weaker than them. Her advantage, if they did not know the perils of dealing with a pirate.

The women, all young and pretty, all companions, flocked and flitted together like birds, eyeing Scarlet as if she were a cat. Scarlet caught a glass of wine from a passing waiter and tossed it off. It spread a pleasant warmth without dulling her wits. And now to work. Bellecombe had hinted at some sort of merchant's club, where deals were done on the quiet. She'd do her deal with all at once, get promises about the slaves, and hopefully find a way to transform all the clutter in the *Donnybrook*'s hold into pure gold.

⌘

Robert eyed the tall, glowing house with deep unease. Though the dowagers of Port Royal had already invited him to every possible social gathering he did not yet feel comfortable at them. His eyes flicked to the dusky lady in her fine clothes. Women. He was not at all sure how he was supposed to treat Tavernier's companion. He hoped there would not be dancing. He could feel Tavernier watching out of the corner of his eye, and was careful to keep his face blank.

He let Stille precede him up the porch and through the wide door. They were late. Robert clenched his jaw, aware that in this place he and Stille represented their home country. He kept his back straight and went into the light.

The servants let them in. The host, grand in a full grey wig and a fine suit of cream silk, exchanged bows with Tavernier and his lady, bows with Stille, and after a brief, curious examination, Robert. Then he turned and presented Robert to his very special guest, Captain Scarlet MacGrath, of the *Donnybrook*.

This woman looked nothing at all like the creature by the docks. The long red hair had been put up in some fantastical way, her skin glowed like ivory, she was dressed like a lady and adorned with pearls.

The pirate smirked as she held out her hand, and after a moment while Robert searched for any other response that propriety allowed, he bent briefly over it and murmured something meaningless. The bow brought him uncomfortably close to her bosom, almost completely bare and jutting forward like that of a ship's figurehead. Several ungentlemanly thoughts raced through his mind, and he took a moment to regain his composure. As he rose up he saw a question in her eyes, and the smirk was gone.

As soon as possible, he retreated to a corner and watched the room. The women present were professionals. They mixed freely with all the men, flirted and looked into eyes, and touched. A few appeared to be slightly aged European beauties. Several appeared to have some African blood.

The men knew each other well. Robert watched as Stille was taken around, introduced. Robert could tell it was business, but to his eye, the business seemed more immediate than Stille's declared goal of establishing social connections.

Through all of this the pirate moved. She did not linger with any of the women, but traveled from one man to another, flirting, laughing, but sometimes speaking earnestly. One moment she pressed the length of her body against Bellecombe, lithe and lusty and immoral as a she-cat. Next she was in earnest talk with a group, meeting eyes, gaining nods of approval. A moment later she was arguing with Tavernier, fist raised, looking as if she would punch or stab the man in a moment. It was like having a wild animal in the room. There was no telling what she would do next.

⌘

"…and she screams, 'No! No! It is not a rat! Worse! It is an Englishman!'"

Scarlet bowed to her audience's laughter, and mentally thanked Flynn, who had made up the joke a week ago. The looks on these men's faces had been slowly changing from appreciation of what lay within her dress to a grudging respect for what she had to say. She raised her glass to them and said, "To new friendships!" The Frenchmen raised their glasses and drank in reply, and Scarlet took the opportunity to lean in and ask in a low voice, "And why did this latest brace of rats come in, d' you think?"

"The same as all Englishmen." A fellow in a pale blue suit and a shirt billowing with lace waved a scented handkerchief as if to dispel a lingering aroma of roast beef. "Trade. From their kings to their beggars, contracts and profits are all they ever think of."

A knowing chuckle went 'round, and Scarlet joined in, but she was looking at the faces. Bellecombe had shown a great deal of curiosity in "unusual objects," and she had never met a rich man who wasn't mighty interested in money, but these Frenchmen seemed to feel that talking about it wasn't proper, which was not going to make her task easier.

The privateer, Tavernier, wandered over, nodded to the others, raised his glass to Scarlet. She looked at him coolly. He came in close, looked at her in a way that made her want to pull up the front of her dress, saw her embarrassment and smiled. She raised her chin, hauled her shoulders back in defiance and smiled back. He took her hand (If she had pulled back there would have been a wrestling match) and kissed it with deep passion. Scarlet held her shoulders still like iron, and felt the change in her whole posture. (Not so stupid, these rich women. The mere tightening of the shoulders, in this rig, could turn one into a creature of ice. Even a creature with Scarlet's hot anger inside.)

Tavernier was angry. She could see it in the line of his upper lip. He came close and whispered something into her ear. She recognized the words, but hadn't been aware that even a Frenchman would try to do such a thing with pig's dung. She replied in her bad French, "My gift to you, also."

He took her arm, forcibly, and let her away from the others, toward the buffet. (Maybe not so smart, these rich women. With the corset imprisoning her body, she had no leverage to pull away.)

Four feet from the intricate display of food, he paused and whispered again, "You little *espèce de connasse*. You are of no consequence. You are a moment's entertainment, no more. Don't pretend to talk to men."

She rounded on him like the *Donnybrook* coming about in battle. "Don't you speak so to me, or I'll have you out in the open sea, and you'll be a sorry jack. I know you. You killed Tommy Blue, and sunk the *Dancing Molly*. I used to go drinkin' with Tommy."

"*Tu es un putain*. You have no idea of men's business.

"You damn privateers, you can't see who's your own kind and who ain't. Goin' out and killin' poor Tommy, and what did he ever do to you? Who told you to do it? I know you don't have the stones to pick a fight on your own."

"*Va te faire mettre!*"

"*Vous êtes une pomme de terre avec le visage d'un cochon d'inde !* Oh, you're surprised I know that one? Well, you do look a sight like a potato, and I should know. Now get your ugly nose out of my face, or I won't wait until you have the guts to go to sea."

The exchange had been low voiced, but folk were starting to look. One of the ladies whispered behind her fan to Tavernier's woman, who went pink. Tavernier glanced about and stalked off with great dignity.

Scarlet got her temper under control with a massive effort and turned blindly to the buffet. She was looking over the food when she realized she had blundered right up against Captain Davenport. From the hot skillet into the bleedin' fire.

⌘

He met her at the punch-bowl, where she held her cup out to the servant, and looked over the food, bold as any man. When she saw him, her face twisted through three or four emotions until it settled on a kind of arch cheerfulness. "So, Bobbie? I didn't expect to see you here. You enjoyin' yourself?"

Looking into her green eyes was like staring into two gun-ports, hot and hostile. She looked as if she wanted to knife him, even as she held back her shoulders, displaying her half-naked breasts. He retreated into icy propriety. "I don't believe I've given you leave to use my Christian name."

"Oh, we're being proper? All right then Captain, ah, Davenport, ain't it? Then you must call me 'Captain MacGuire.'

Too bad, I was going to ask you to call me 'Scarlet'. I know you have my name, it's on all the 'Wanted' bills."

How could anyone speak so casually about being a thief? But she had at least retreated on the matter of his name. Perhaps he could force another retreat. He stepped in close, as carefully as if approaching a panther, and looked down at her, willing her to comply. Aloud he said, "Since we are both guests of the same gentleman, we should make some effort to have pleasant conversation."

Her head went back like a skittish horse, and the expression in her eyes changed to wary consideration. The green eyes darted from side to side. He could actually see her thinking.

⌘

Scarlet looked up into his blue eyes and willed herself not to take a step back. She had never been so close to a Navy captain. The man had brought his will and authority to bear on her, and she found it an almost physical force. Here was a ship's captain who had never been forced to persuade, cajole or bargain with a crew. When he ordered a thing, he expected to see it done, be it raising a sail or beating a man to death.

Her Irish temper did not like this kind of authority. She felt rage starting again, drained off a punch-cup (good rum watered with fruit until it was pallid as beer) and dropped the empty onto the table. She had no idea how to reply to his invitation to be civil. She didn't want civility, she wanted flight or battle. He was staring at her as if she was some sort of interesting insect. Almost against her will, she clenched her hand into a fist.

Someone swept up beside them, and Scarlet was vaguely aware that it was Tavernier's woman. She heard a flutter of French, caught the words 'lovely couple' and 'dance' and felt herself propelled into the middle of the room, just as the musicians in the corner struck up a minuet.

Tavernier stepped out and took the lady's hand, and Scarlet was left with the Englishman. Damn them. They didn't think she could dance, and thought to make a fool of her. Well, she had done this one a few times. Every damned merchant seemed to know the minuet, if no other. She rustled her skirt by way of a curtsy and began to move to the music.

The steps had never made much sense to her. A series of circling patterns, the man and the woman apart, coming closer and closer together, until at the last moment, almost touching, they pulled away and went back to the beginning without ever brushing figures.

It felt more natural in a grand dress, and she could not help but notice that the man's part showed off Robert Davenport's coat and calves to advantage. Not a bad looking man at all, but still one she would relish having at the end of a cutlass. She had never danced in anger before, but just now, angry at two men at the same time, the grand dress became as sails, and Scarlet a sloop sailing out to do battle. She held the English captain's eyes, and to her surprise he made no effort to look away, staring as if to drive her to submission.

They were fencers, circling for advantage, ships in combat striving for the weather gage, a navy captain and a pirate, dancing a dance of battle and retreat. The first time they reached the center of the pattern, his hand actually reached for her, against the whole form of the dance, and she barely avoided his grasping fingers. In the next repetition of pattern she held his eyes, daring him to try it again.

She could imagine the rope in his hands, his desire to put it around her neck, and felt a deep exhilaration that life still ran through her, in spite of him and all his kind. She smiled an animal grin, with teeth. This time when his hand reached, she teased him by letting her fingers play between his.

130

Once again she escaped, retreating gracefully to the outer ring of the dance. Their eyes were locked. She could see the anger in him, and feel her own burning until it seemed the dress must go up in flames. It was the final pattern. She had the option of letting him catch her. As the music ended she held out her fingers, waited half a heartbeat, then twisted her wrist and grasped his hand, controlling it. His eyes widened with surprise. Then he stepped in and covered her fingers with his left hand. She was caught.

He held her like iron fetters, and let his right arm stray to a position around her waist, moving her toward the open French doors and out onto the balcony.

⌘

Robert had never felt this way before. He was outraged, insulted, intrigued, aroused. The creature in his arms was fire, ice and gunpowder and he held her with due care, for he knew she was very dangerous. Outside, away from the candle smoke and the heavy smell of perfumes and food, he let his arm drop away from her waist and, holding her hand tight, spun her roughly around to face him. "Kindly explain what you are doing here, Madame."

She stared into his eyes, stuck out her chin and said, "I come in to buy slaves off these men. Let go of me."

He did not loosen his grip at all. "Don't think you can make me believe that. Slaves are sold to plantations, not the other way round. What would make you do something so stupid?"

"What would make me?" the rage on her face was so strong he could scarcely keep himself from taking a step back. "Only that you rum bastards are off selling my people for slaves again! Draggin' folk from their homes for no damn reason. This lot to die in the French cane fields, instead of on your bloody Barbados. I wonder you can live with yourself."

"What are you talking about?"

131

"You know. You damn well know. You're with that bloody-handed East India slave dealer, and him making a fortune off stealing my people, I don't doubt. How much are they paying you to kidnap children and priests?"

Robert threw her hand down in annoyance. "You are mad or misinformed. The Irish slave trade died with Cromwell. You're a subject of the Crown, not some savage to be sold at auction."

"I ain't subject to no one or nothing, and there's boats full of Irish comin' into the Carib every day." She spat on the clean tiles of the balcony. "*That* for what you know."

He took a step back and looked at her closely. She meant it, outrage bristled from every pore and her blazing eyes never wavered. Then in a burst of light, it all made sense. Stille's odd mission to sell slaves to the French, when English plantations were buying up as many as could be brought. Tavernier had smoothed the way, perhaps.

The East India Company had its own battleships, it was no stretch to imagine them with an army. The Irish had been battered to pieces for years. Kidnapping country peasants, even by the shipload, would not excite much attention, and they were not equipped to fight back.

And, last of all, his own presence. A tacit hint that the British government knew and approved. A lie, but apparently Stille had no shame, and nerves of steel. Illegally kidnapping Irish at no cost and selling them as slaves for pure profit could bring in a fortune.

Obviously it must stop. Robert wondered how to begin on that. It would be an enormous case, treason, perhaps. The government and the East India Company in conflict, careers brought down, men hanged. All on the word of a pirate.

He shook his head. "It makes sense. But in order to do anything I will need proof. Can you offer any?"

She paused and looked at him in question. "What do you mean? I thought you was on their side. You're with 'em."

Robert did not want her to associate him in any way with Stille and his vile trade. "I mean stop it, if it's really happening. If it is *really* happening. But I haven't seen anything. Do you have proof?"

"What are you driving at?" Scarlet knew he was lying, but she couldn't think of why he would. She kept both eyes on him, looking for the lie.

He gazed into her eyes for a long time, so long that she began to think he would try to kiss her. He never moved, but finally said, "You believe this is happening. I think you may be right, and I may be able to stop it. I need facts to send to my superiors. If you have any, it would help."

Scarlet frowned. "What are Irish peasants to you?"

"It's against the law."

She waited for the rest of it. He offered nothing else, and she tested the idea that a law could benefit someone. Finally, very deliberately, she said, "You'll pardon me, but the law ain't never come down on my side before. How do I know things won't change?"

He frowned and stepped toward her again. "Selling slaves out of Ireland was legal once, but that was during radical times. Those times are over. A rightful king is back on the throne, and I will do my best to enforce His Majesty's wishes. But understand me; piracy is, was, and ever will be illegal."

Scarlet smiled to herself. A liar, she reckoned, would have promised more. She had guessed right, this one was honorable. The man beside her smelled warm and male, with a faint undertone of rum, and the sea.

She decided it was worth a little risk. "I have your proof, I think. A Dutch ship's logbook, as carried Irish slaves. Captain didn't know he was doin' wrong, the log likely gives names and such. I don't read Dutch. Would it do?"

Robert closed his eyes for a moment. "You can't come onboard my ship, it's part of England. Can you get the book to me by messenger?"

"I ain't got it, but I know where it is…"

"Is everything well with you, Mademoiselle Scarlet?" Bellecombe stepped onto the balcony. He gave Davenport an annoyed glance, and murmured in French, "The barbarian did not…"

Scarlet smiled. "The gentleman was faint from the dance, and needed air."

Bellecombe smiled, looked at Robert and then laughed out loud. "I hope you are feeling better now, *Capitaine*?" The English captain smiled and gave Scarlet a gesture very like a salute.

She nodded graciously and let Bellecombe lead her back to the party.

A plate of food, another glass of wine. Bellecombe was suddenly attentive. "I have very good news for you. My friends have been considering… one or two things. I believe you can collect your slaves within a day or two. Where do you think we should have them brought?"

"I think the slave market has a place. All your friends, you say? How did you bring 'em around so quick?"

"You made the point, *mon cheri*. These people were sold as barbarians. Most of them spoke no language we could understand, and, since they came from the Dutch and English, we never thought they shared a church with us. You are right, we are concerned. It is easier to accept your generous offer. A few runners have been sent out, and more will go in the morning. If you would care to send a message to your ship, perhaps we can look for exotic objects tomorrow? There are places near the slave yard where goods can be unloaded."

"I'll be goin' back to my ship to sleep." He pouted, and she put a finger to his lips. "I told you, business first."

She had been tracking the English captain with half an eye, and was aware that his fat companion was spluttering and carrying on. Good. If that fellow was pissed off, she felt all the safer. Perhaps Robert Davenport had been telling the truth. Dealing with him would be a fine, dangerous game. But she would never trust him, no matter how handsome his calves.

A couple came up to wish Bellecombe a good evening, and Scarlet sent a maid to ask Pryce to gather all the discarded clothes and have the carriage brought around.

She spent some considerable time pressing the hands of the various French, thanking them for their efforts in freeing good Catholics. Her relief that this complex, exhausting evening was drawing to a close apparently made her seem sincere. She drew a little knot of slave-owners, who looked into her eyes, not merely down the front of her dress. Even their expensive companions seemed more curious, less hostile.

Her host walked her to the carriage, offering one passionate kiss in the dark. She climbed in smiling to herself.

Pryce sat opposite her, the box across her lap. "You look glad. Did the deal go well?"

"I think we'll have it done some time tomorrow. But I want to spend a few more days, provisioning up and enjoying the pleasures of the port."

"Pleasures of the port." Pryce's smile showed in her voice, though away from the house's lantern, the dark clung too tight to see. "Was it Tavernier? I thought I saw him get in a carriage, just before you came out. Flashy devil."

Scarlet tried to sit back, but the stays held her stiff as a board. "The man was there, but he's an ass. No, it's the host I've a mind to visit."

"He has a good reputation with his servants. What about that Navy captain? Flynn had quite a story about you meeting him in the street. I never thought you'd sit down to dinner with one of 'em."

"Nor did I." The image of Robert Davenport's angry blue eyes swam agreeably into her mind and she smiled to herself.

The carriage jounced along, past houses and over streets of mud and stone. Then the pleasant, regular clatter of the horse's hooves went irregular and the carriage lurched, jerked and came to a stop. Pryce swore and stuck her head out the window. "What the devil?"

The carriage jerked again as the driver jumped down, and they were treated to a flood of French, with swearwords. Pryce banged open the door and clambered out, trailing skirts. Scarlet heard swearing in English and climbed out after her. Houses lined the road at irregular intervals, but the lanterns at their doors had gone dark. A glance at the stars told her it was about two in the morning.

The coachman was on his knees in the road, looking at one of the port horse's feet. He reached to lift it, and the animal snorted and jerked away.

Pryce translated. "He says it tripped over something and hurt itself." The coachman made another try at the foot, and the horse jerked again, staggered, and stumbled into its teammate. That animal shied and kicked. The coachman grabbed the trailing rein and held the team back. When he looked up his face seemed sickly yellow under the light of the carriage's running lamp. He spoke again and Scarlet caught it, but Pryce translated anyway. "The carriage is goin' nowhere. This horse can't pull, and the other can't do the job alone."

"No trouble." Scarlet patted the man's shoulder. "We won't... Pryce, tell the man we won't beat him or complain to his employer."

Pryce rattled off something and dug out a coin. "He says he can't leave the carriage here."

"Well, I ain't afraid to walk back to the ship. You have a pistol?" Pryce nodded. "You got all the knives out of my kit? Good. Then I will take a moment to put on my French boots, and we will walk to the pier."

Pryce dragged the box out under the lamp, and Scarlet rooted through it and hauled out the boots. Putting them on with the stays holding her was impossible, so she sat in the carriage's open doorway, and Pryce knelt down and slid them up, hauling Scarlet's skirts to the thigh.

"I don't believe I am doing this," Pryce muttered, as the leather stuck at Scarlet's knees, and the coachman strained mightily to see. "You have good shoes, those are my Chinese-silk shoes, and it ain't a mile to the pier."

"I am protecting your shoes from getting muddy, and my boots from getting stolen. I don't mind being knifed in an alley, or robbed, but no one is getting these boots."

"You had better not get knifed, that's my dress you have on, and I mean to wear it."

"If you would only..."

Another carriage rolled up, bringing lantern light and the shadows of horses. The two coachmen exchanged words, and the carriage door opened. The first man out was Tavernier. The second was the bloody English slave dealer, and the third was Robert Davenport. Scarlet tossed her skirt over her knees and stood, scowling.

Davenport drew his eyebrows together in distress as he saw Scarlet, then stepped around to look at Pryce. Scarlet saw his concern and laughed to herself. "Fool thinks she's really some servant-girl I picked up in port."

Tavernier stepped forward. "Why are we hanging about here? There is nothing to be done. We cannot take anyone else on, the carriage is full."

Robert turned back to him, but his eyes flicked to Pryce. "In all honor, then, aren't we bound to turn the carriage over to the ladies, and walk?"

The fat one began to protest, but Tavernier, his eyes glittering in the moonlight, waved a hand a cut him off. "No, no. The gentleman is correct. These ladies must ride. But to send them off with no male escort would be almost as bad as leaving them here. As I have a companion to escort, I believe I will take up the task. You gentlemen are agreeable?"

Robert replied, "Yes," immediately, while the fat one spluttered again.

Scarlet had to admit, it was gallant, especially if the woman he was protecting appeared to be only a maid. She met his eyes and gave a gracious nod before saying to Tavernier, "That's right kind of you. Do you mind dropping us off at my ship?"

Tavernier murmured socially correct and utterly insulting things about the helplessness of women, and Robert took a moment to ask Pryce if she felt safe. She nodded, gathering up the spilled bits of costume, and joined Scarlet in the carriage.

The interior was dark, upholstered in leather, and exactly the right size to accommodate four passengers, two in extravagant dresses. As they clattered along, smooth on expensive springs, Tavernier's lady put up her fan and whispered something that included the word "*gauche.*"

"You can say it to my face," Scarlet replied. "I don't much care."

Tavernier's eyes glittered in the dark. "I need to say nothing about you. You are nothing but a trollop."

"Then why're you at such pains to say so?"

"Stay away from my friends. I've warned them about you. It is not necessary to commit a crime in order to run afoul of the authorities here."

"I'll be sure to tell Charles when he comes tomorrow to sell me them slaves."

For a minute the carriage was quiet except for Tavernier's hard, angry breathing. Then he reached up and knocked hard on the carriage roof, signaling the driver to stop. Almost before the wheels had ceased rolling, he caught Scarlet by the hand and dragged her into the street.

After the near-total darkness of the coach, the street seemed bright as morning. Tavernier jerked Scarlet close and she let him. She could smell the wine on his breath, see how his neck cloth had wilted and his wig had fallen askew. Without the heavy curls, she could also see a jagged scar along his jaw. She followed it back with her eyes to the left ear, cut away years ago.

"You poor bastard," she whispered. "Goin' through all this shite to hang about with the quality, and you never will be one of 'em, no more'n me. We're both an afternoon's amusement, only you, poor sod, you care."

Tavernier exploded with words that dripped venom, then pulled a hidden knife. Scarlet tried to catch his wrist, but the stays didn't let her body turn, and her trailing sleeves hampered her. She backed two paces, stepped onto the edge of the skirt and trapped herself.

He came in fast, and she bloodied her fingers trying to stop the blade, but he slammed the knife into her with his full weight behind it.

She gasped as he drew back to strike again. Then the hiss-bang of a pistol rang out from beside the carriage. Tavernier jerked as the shot hit, gave a high-pitched shriek and fell.

Scarlet didn't wait to see if he stayed down. She lifted her skirt up and heeled it back to the carriage, where Pryce stood with the smoking pistol in her hand. "Come on!" Scarlet called, and headed downhill toward the pier, cutting through a flower garden on her way.

Pryce caught Scarlet on the next street. "Are you all right?"

"Well enough." She gestured toward the box in Pryce's hand. "Silk shoes?"

"Yes. Damn. I've stepped in…"

"Glad you ain't wearing 'em?"

They made good time, and avoided any cut-throats insomniac enough to be out. At the head of the pier Scarlet dropped her skirts, and swept onto the *Donnybrook* like a lady, enjoying the surprised expression on the lookout's face. "Hello Darby. Thanks, Flynn, for your good work. I think we'll see slaves brought in tomorrow. Now, should a man in a black shirt and coat come to the ship, kindly shoot him. He's tried to kill your captain this night."

Pryce followed Scarlet into the aft cabin, grumbling. "You think I didn't kill him?"

"It was too dark to see, and a tough shot. Now get me out of this damn dress."

⌘

This was the second time he had watched that pirate drive away in a carriage.

By Robert's side, Stille complained loudly about pirates, women, and Navy captains who could not put their damn regulations aside for one moment.

Robert turned on him at last. "Sir. You have requested my presence for *your* damn negotiations, and this evening's efforts have failed. I am not your lap-dog. If you continue to treat my office with this level of disrespect, I will have you out on the field of honor. Do you take my meaning, sir?"

Stille's abrupt silence conveyed his understanding, and for a moment, Robert closed his eyes and listened to the quiet and the soft sound of the moving sea. Then he began to walk.

He hoped the maid would be all right. The pirate, he was sure, would survive anything. Dancing with her had been... He had never quite understood the point of dancing before. All he had ever thought about was putting his feet in the right place and remembering what figure he was on. His sincere desire to throttle the woman had blown that uncertainty aside like a cannon blast.

And this business with the slaves. She had been ready enough to accuse Stille, and he had to admit the man did not make a good impression, but to imagine some sort of conspiracy to kidnap Crown subjects and sell them into slavery was far-fetched at the least.

Near the docks, the naked masts rose like a winter forest. Stille's *Boulder* rocked gently next to the *Nightingale*, and as Robert approached, he wondered idly where the *Donnybrook* lay and what would happen if he wandered over for a visit. His eyes darted over his ship, her masts towering over nearly everything in the harbor.

A real thought came, that he should climb up and inspect the shrouds tomorrow. If he timed it right, he might just be able to catch another good look at Scarlet MacGrath, and see what she was really doing at the slave yard.

That decided, he went quietly aboard. Hughes was waiting up for him, with a fresh nightshirt and a cup of rosemary tea in precaution for the headache Robert would undoubtedly have tomorrow, and Robert's book beside his chair.

With the heavy uniform and the stiff wig peeled off at last, it should have been a pleasure to sit and simply look out the stern window at the water. But pirates and privateers kept maneuvering through his head. One pirate in particular. How had she learned to dance that way?

⌘

Pryce found a knife and cut the stitches she had closed the dress's back with, then helped peel the thing off Scarlet's arms. "It wasn't that dark, and I swear I saw him knife you. And here you are, right as rain. Not a drop of blood."

"I don't think it was a proper blade. More one of those Italian stilettos. I scratched my hand on it, trying to turn it off, but the bleeding's stopped already." She held up her fingers.

"Damned thing." Pryce cut the stay-laces and the stiff form fell from Scarlet's body so abruptly her flesh hurt.

"Mother of Jesus," Scarlet said as she passed a hand over her side. "I'm galled all along my ribs. I'll never get into one of those again!"

"It would be easier if it fit you." Pryce carried the garment to a lamp to see better. "Well, there's our mystery." She held the stays out for Scarlet's inspection. "Look there, the wooden slat caught the blade. Not so angry at 'em now, eh?"

"Still pretty poor armor." Stripped down to her chemise, Scarlet sat and put her boot heels up on her desk, digging in the bottom drawer for a bottle and mugs. "Here, have a tot of whisky. Dry in the servant's hall?"

"Very dry." Pryce unhooked the front of her dress as Scarlet poured. "And did I hear you say slaves delivered tomorrow?"

"So they tell me."

"Will we be able to pay for all of them?"

Scarlet closed her eyes and imagined for a moment a barefoot woman, standing on the dock, still a slave because the *Donnybrook* had run out of funds. "I have a bit in cash. My own store. I think it will do."

Pryce looked at her sideways, but said only, "Mighty fine trading."

Robert Davenport had wandered into Scarlet's thoughts, but she dragged them back to Bellecombe, with his elegant home and his overlarge nose. "I frightened him with hell, offered cash, and used the weapons you gave me. Bellecombe asks me back to dine. I'm sure it will be fish and frogs, but the rose arbor is said to be beautiful, and he has promised to show me."

"To rose arbors, then"

That damned English captain was still in Scarlet's mind, but she raised her glass and echoed, "To rose arbors

The End

But wait, there's more!

The next book in The Pirate Empire

Chapter 1

Moskito Coast...

"And what was it made you think I'd take in more lost sheep?" This time Conner Donnelly gave no pretense of greeting honored guests. His best coat was somewhere else, and his shirt sleeves were rolled to the elbow. Scarlet considered it a victory that she had made her way as far as his office. The four slaves who had rowed ashore with her still stood on the beach, with Burgess and Dark Maire bracketing them and Conner's brother Sean holding them all at gunpoint.

Scarlet licked her lips. "It's a hot day, love. Give us a pint of beer?"

"I will not. Your last lot are drinking it as fast as we can make it. And eating us right off the beach."

"No grand thing goes easy. You know that. But your city's going up. What's that lovely structure back on the hill?"

Conner's eyes flashed. "It's a church, if you can't tell from the great cross they've raised up beside it. A bloody church, because you had to bring me a bloody priest..." His voice had been rising, and he cut himself off suddenly and looked around, before continuing in a much softer tone. "As if I didn't have work and danger on every side, food to be caught and ships to be sunk, and natives watching us from the woods. Now I have a Holy Father with no confidence in my means of livelihood or the state of my soul."

Scarlet leaned in and whispered. "And what was I supposed to do with him? Throw him into the ocean? Hand him over to Ned Doyle?"

At mention of Doyle, Conner shut his eyes for a moment, but when he opened them he did not seem more sociable. "The priest wants to reform me."

"A cooper wants to sell barrels. That don't mean you have to buy 'em."

"He's a priest, and his flock is with him. It ain't easy." Conner sighed. "The man's pretty damn close to getting control of this stretch of beach clean away from me. I may have to move."

"Conner, not that!"

"I tell you, the last time we set out a signal fire, the good father walked down the beach and put it out. Mick hauled him off, but then all those folk with him was angry. They're like to drive us all off our own land."

Scarlet shifted uneasily. "Have you spoken to the man?"

"A priest? If it's so easy, why don't you do it?"

"Well, he was on my ship four days. I do know him a bit."

Conner stood and leaned over the desk, hovering over Scarlet, his shoulders looming. "You get the good father calmed down, and I'll think about taking on this next lot. Not before."

Scarlet looked at her knuckles for a while, glanced up

at Conner and finally said, "As you will." She had never argued with a priest before.

It was a long, hot tramp back into the brush, the air still and the path clogged with palmetto fronds that tore at Scarlet's clothes and skin. She found her way by keeping an eye up to the rough tower with its looming cross, taller than the great trees that surrounded it.

The work site was cleared of trees and brush, and Scarlet paused for a moment in the last of the forest's shade before going on. She wished she could shed some clothes, but it did not seem a wise choice when going to talk to a priest. Instead, she unpinned her skirt and let it fall to its full length, covering her ankles. Then she stepped out into the glare.

She found Father Patrick standing on a pile of dirt while those around him rested, hiding from the blistering sun under scrub trees and palms. He had contrived a rough black cassock from somewhere, and a silver cross hung on his chest. He had covered his head with a wide straw hat, but his face was burned red. Scarlet dropped a curtsey, and looked into his eyes. Fierce enough, but with no taint of sunstroke or madness.

"Yes, Captain MacGrath?"

"I've come to speak to you, Father, about your situation." Out in the sun, the heat was worse. Sweat ran down Scarlet's neck and between her breasts.

"What?" Father Patrick swatted at a mosquito. "We're raising a church here, to show our gratitude to God and dig ourselves into this new land."

"And may I ask what else are your parishioners doing? Folk cannot eat a church."

"We have built homes. The women plant and gather.

146

This new land is bountiful." He shifted, looking down from his pile of dirt.

Scarlet swallowed. It was most unpleasant to look up at him, with the pale sky like white-hot iron behind. "And do you help to man the cannons by the cove mouth?" she asked. "Do you trade?"

"We have not come to that yet."

"Nor will you. It's a matter for the governor of this land."

At this Father Patrick came down off his dirt, wiped his forehead with a cloth and stared at her, making her sweat even more. "What? That boy? He is a pirate and a murderer. He lights false signal-fires along the coast, and means to wreck passing ships. He'll bring the law or the wrath of God down upon us all."

A tart remark rose to Scarlet's lips, but she held it back. Instead, she dropped her eyes, then looked up slowly. "It seems to me, Father, that we do our share of good. You was all saved for that we took that ship of yours as a prize."

"It was God's hand moving you, lass. And now I need to bring the same upon these barbarians."

Scarlet could remember the results of other false signal fires, the dead bodies washing up on the beach. She sighed. "He does it because he need to, Father. It ain't like he enjoys it."

"And that cleans his soul? What about the women these scamps chase, or... " Father Patrick paused and looked sharply up the trail that Scarlet had come by. A little girl, her hair in braids, her skirt and blouse apparently made from some of Conner's trade silk, came running up. "Father," she curtsied, then paused, looking frightened. "Conner says to bring everyone back to the shore."

"And now the young villain is ordering me about!" The priest pounded a fist into his left palm and glared at Scarlet as if she was somehow responsible for Conner.

Scarlet was looking at the girl, who stood on one bare foot, rubbing her ankle on the back of the opposite calf. "What's all the rush?"

The girl looked nervously between Scarlet and the priest. "I don't know, mum. His brother Mick came in from the forest and then he sent me to bring you."

The priest was beginning to turn turkey red in the face, and Scarlet raised a placating hand. "Father, this don't seem like Conner's regular way of doing business. Give the man a chance and come in. Besides, it's hot as... hot enough to... hot enough to fry an egg on a stone, it is. Come back to the shore and have a drink.

One of the laborers, sitting on a fallen tree, called out, "It's fearsome hot, Father, and we could all stand with a drink."

Scarlet did her best to be persuasive without flirting. "The surf's cool and the sea breeze is blowing. Your men can't do no more work 'til sunset, or they'll drop like flies. Get 'em someplace cool."

"All right, all right." Father Patrick glared at Scarlet, but took off his straw hat and waved it to the lounging worker. They gathered up their gear so quickly that Scarlet suspected they'd been looking for an excuse for some time.

Scarlet was first back to the beach, but the scene was much different from when she had walked away from it an hour ago. Now the huts, the shade-tress and the beach itself were crowded with people. A quick glance told her that they could be none but the former slaves. When she had seen them last they had been pale and thin, their clothes stained from their confinement. Now they were tanned and freckled by the sun, wearing odd combinations of sailcloth, trade silk and Indian cotton. Men, women and children, they crowded Conner's settlement like ants on a hill.

She pushed her way through the crowd and finally found Conner, standing with Mick halfway into the jungle. "What the devil's up?"

"Natives." Conner held a long rifle, and Mick was bleeding from a wound on his head. "They attacked Mick in the woods."

"I didn't give 'em no cause to fire first, but I did fire after." Mick glared at Scarlet as if she had accused him of something. "Bastards just shot me out of nowhere. We fired back, and I think we got one."

"You should have tried talking." Conner looked from Mick to Scarlet, his brow furrowed. "The locals are pretty friendly, mostly. We trade with 'em. They've never offered to fight before, even when there's been arguments about women and such."

"What did you do to them?" Scarlet demanded, looking at Mick.

"Not a thing. We were hunting wild pigs. We do it all the time. They just shot me, and yelled something, and run off."

"What are natives doing with guns?" Scarlet glared at Mick.

"They've always had, 'em," Conner said. "They had a few when we came here, and we've traded them for more. A musket's worth twenty goats or fifteen pigs."

Scarlet gaped at him. "You've given guns to a lot of savages?"

Conner turned on her. "They ain't savages. They're folks, and they've been right good to us. Speak English, and anxious to trade fair. They ain't been like this before."

"Well they're like this now!" Mick waved his fist in Conner's face. "Will you give me a bigger party to go out and deal with 'em or not?"

Conner opened his mouth to reply, but the sharp "pang!" of a gunshot rang out in the distance and he paused. Scarlet stood beside him, watching and listening, as something came toward them, crashing and ripping through the brush. Conner pulled a pistol from his belt, and Scarlet reached into her coat pockets for her own guns.

It was a heard or a tribe or a mob. Scarlet could hear their footsteps and their occasional cries. From further back in the brush more gunshots rang out. Mick pulled a knife with a jagged, ugly blade, and Conner turned the hunting rifle in his hands to wield it like a club.

...to be continued.

Be sure to enjoy
The next installment in The Pirate Empire

Bloody Seas

Book reviews are the best way to let an author know how you feel about their work. If you enjoyed this book (or if you didn't!) please be sure to log onto Amazon and add your review.

Made in the USA
San Bernardino, CA
09 November 2018